THE BARON'S GLOVES

OR
AMY'S ROMANCE

LOUISA MAY ALCOTT

ELM HILL BOOKS
A Division of Thomas Nelson Publishers
Since 1798

www.thomasnelson.com

The Baron's Gloves
ISBN: 1404186166

The quoted ideas expressed in this book (but not scripture verses) are not, in all
cases, exact quotations, as some have been edited for clarity and brevity. In all
cases, the author has attempted to maintain the speaker's original intent. In some
cases, quoted material for this book was obtained from secondary sources, primari-
ly print media. While every effort was made to ensure the accuracy of these
sources, the accuracy cannot be guaranteed. For additions, deletions, corrections or
clarifications in future editions of this text, please e-mail
ContactUs@ElmHillBooks.com.

Products from Elm Hill Books may be purchased in bulk for educational, business,
fundraising, or sales promotional use. For information, please email
SpecialMarkets@ThomasNelson.com.

Cover design: Patti Evans
Interior: Jennifer Ross

"All is fair in love and war."

I
How They Were Found

"What a long sigh! Are you tired, Amy?"

"Yes, and disappointed as well. I never would have undertaken this journey if I had not thought it would be full of novelty, romance, and charming adventures."

"Well, we have had several adventures."

"Bah! Losing one's hat in the Rhine, getting left at a dirty little inn, and having our pockets picked, are not what I call adventures. I wish there were brigands in Germany—it needs something of that sort to enliven its stupidity."

"How can you call Germany stupid when you have a scene like this before you?" said Helen, with a sigh of pleasure, as she looked from the balcony which overhangs the Rhine at the hotel of the 'Three Kings' at Coblentz. Ehrenbreitstein towered opposite, the broad river glittered below, and a midsummer moon lent its enchantment to the landscape.

As she spoke, her companion half rose from the low chair where she lounged, and showed the pretty, piquant face of a young girl. She seemed in a half melancholy, half petulant mood; and traces of recent illness were visible in the languor of her movements and the pallor of her cheeks.

"Yes, it is lovely; but I want adventures and romance of some sort to make it quite perfect. I don't care what, if something would only happen."

"My dear, you are out of spirits and weary now, tomorrow you'll be yourself again. Do not be ungrateful to uncle or unjust to yourself. Something pleasant will happen; I've no doubt. In fact, something has happened that you may make a little romance out of, perhaps, for lack of a more thrilling adventure."

"What do you mean?" and Amy's listless face brightened.

"Speak low; there are balconies all about us, and we may be overheard," said Helen, drawing nearer after an upward glance.

"What is the beginning of a romance?" whispered Amy, eagerly.

"A pair of gloves. Just now, as I stood here, and you lay with your eyes shut, these dropped from the balcony overhead. Now amuse yourself by weaving a romance out of them and their owner."

Amy seized them and, stepping inside the window, examined them by the candle.

"A gentleman's gloves, scented with violets! Here's a little hole fretted by a ring on the third finger. Bless me! Here are the initials, 'S.P.,' stamped on the inside, with a coat of arms below. What a fop to get up his gloves in this style! They are exquisite, though. Such a delicate color, so little soiled, and so prettily ornamented! Handsome hands wore these. I'd like to see the man."

Helen laughed at the girl's interest, and was satisfied if any trifle amused her ennui.

"I will send them back by the kellner, and in that way we may discover their owner," she said.

But Amy arrested her on the way to the door.

"I've a better plan; these waiters are so stupid you'll get nothing out of them. Here's the hotel book sent up for our names; let us look among the day's arrivals and see who 'S.P.' is. He came today, I'm sure, for the man said the rooms above were just taken, so we could not have them."

Opening the big book, Amy was soon intently poring over the long list of names, written in many hands and many languages.

"I've got it! Here he is—oh, Nell, he's a baron! Isn't that charming? 'Sigismund von Palsdorf, Dresden.' We must see him, for I know he's handsome, if he wears such distracting gloves."

"You'd better take them up yourself, then."

"You know I can't do that; but I shall ask the man a few questions, just to get an idea what sort of person the baron is. Then I shall change my mind and go down to dinner; shall look well about me, and if the baron is agreeable, I shall make uncle return the gloves. He will thank us, and I can say I've known a real baron. That will be so nice when we go home. Now, don't be duennaish and say I'm silly, but let me do as I like, and come and dress."

Helen submitted, and when the gong pealed through the house, Major Erskine marched into the great *sale a manger*, with a comely niece on each arm. The long tables were crowded, and they had to run the gauntlet of many eyes as they made their way to the head of the upper table. Before she touched her soup, Amy glanced down the line of faces opposite, and finding none that answered the slight description elicited from the waiter, she leaned a little forward to examine those on her own side of the table. Some way down sat several gentlemen, and, as she bent to observe them, one did the same, and she received an admiring glance from a pair of fine black eyes. Somewhat abashed, she busied herself with her soup; but the fancy had taken possession of her, and presently she whispered to Helen—

"Do you see any signs of the baron?"

"On my left; look at the hands."

Amy looked and saw a white, shapely hand with an antique ring on the third finger. Its owner's face was averted, but as he conversed with animation, the hand was in full play, now emphasizing an opinion, now lifting a glass, or more frequently pulling at a blond beard which adorned the face of the unknown. Amy shook her head decidedly.

"I hate light men, and don't think that is the baron, for the gloves are a size too small for those hands. Lean back and look some four or five seats lower down on the right. See what sort of person the dark man with the fine eyes is."

Helen obeyed, but almost instantly bent to her plate again, smiling in spite of herself.

"That is an Englishman; he stares rudely, says 'By Jove!' and wears no jewelry or beard."

"Now, I'm disappointed. Well, keep on the watch, and tell me if you make any discoveries, for I will find the baron."

Being hungry, Amy devoted herself to her dinner, till dessert was on the table. She was languidly eating grapes, while Helen talked with the major, when the word baron caught her ear. The speakers sat at a table behind her, so that she could not see them without turning quite round, which was impossible; but she listened eagerly to the following scrap of chat:

"Is the baron going on tomorrow?" asked a gay voice in French.

"Yes, he is bound for Baden-Baden. The season is at its height, and he must make his game while the ball is rolling, or it is all up with the open-minded Sigismund," answered a rough voice.

"Won't his father pardon the last escapade?" asked a third, with a laugh.

"No, and he is right. The duel was a bad affair, for the man almost died, and the baron barely managed to get out of the scrape through court influence. When is the wedding to be?"

"Never, Palsdorf says. There is everything but love in the bargain, and he swears he'll not agree to it. I like that."

"There is much nobleness in him, spite of his vagaries. He will sow his wild oats and make a grand man in time. By the by, if we are going to the fortress, we must be off. Give Sigismund the word; he is dining at the other table with Power," said the gay voice.

"Take a look at the pretty English girl as you go by;

it will do your eyes good, after the fat Frauleins we have seen of late," added the rough one.

Three gentlemen rose, and as they passed Amy stole a glance at them; but seeing several pairs of eyes fixed on herself, she turned away blushing, with the not unpleasant consciousness that "the pretty English girl" was herself. Longing to see who Sigismund was, she ventured to look after the young men, who paused behind the man with the blond beard, and also touched the dark-eyed gentleman on the shoulder. All five went down the hall and stood talking near the door.

"Uncle, I wish to go," said Amy, whose will was law to the amiable major. Up he rose, and Amy added, as she took his arm, "I'm seized with a longing to go to Baden-Baden and see a little gambling. You are not a wild young man, so you can be trusted there."

"I hope so. Now you are a sensible little woman, and we'll do our best to have a fine time. Wait an instant till I get my hat."

While the major searched for the missing article, the girls went on, and coming to the door, Amy tried to open it. The unwieldy foreign lock resisted her efforts, and she was just giving it an impatient little shake, when a voice said behind her—

"Permit me, mademoiselle;" at the same moment a handsome hand turned the latch, the flash of a diamond shone before her, and the door opened.

"Merci, monsieur," she murmured, turning as she went out; but Helen was close behind her, and no one else to be seen except the massive major in the rear.

"Did you see the baron?" she whispered eagerly, as they went upstairs.

"No; where was he?"

"He opened the door for me. I knew him by his hand and ring. He was close to you."

"I did not observe him, being busy gathering up my dress. I thought the person was a waiter, and never looked at him," said Helen, with provoking indifference.

"How unfortunate! Uncle, you are going to see the fortress; we don't care for it; but I want you to take these gloves and inquire for Baron Sigismund Palsdorf. He will be there with a party of gentlemen. You can easily manage it, men are so free and easy. Mind what his is like, and come home in time to tell me all about it."

Away went the major, and the cousins sat on the balcony enjoying the lovely night, admiring the picturesque scene, and indulging in the flights of fancy all girls love, for Helen, in spite of her three-and-twenty years, was as romantic as Amy at eighteen. It was past eleven when the major came, and the only greeting he received was the breathless question—

"Did you find him?"

"I found something much better than any baron, a courier. I've wanted one ever since we started; for two young ladies and their baggage are more than one man can do his duty by. Karl Hoffman had such excellent testimonials from persons I know, that I did not hesitate to engage him, and he comes tomorrow; so henceforth I've nothing to do but devote myself to you."

"How very provoking! Did you bring the gloves back?" asked Amy, still absorbed in the baron.

The major tossed them to her, and indulged in a hearty laugh at her girlish regrets; then bade them goodnight, and went away to give orders for an early start next morning.

Tired of talking, the girls lay down in the two little white beds always found in German hotels, and Amy was soon continuing in sleep the romance she had begun awake. She dreamed that the baron proved to be the owner of the fine eyes; that he wooed and won her, and they were floating down the river to the chime of wedding-bells.

THE BARON'S GLOVES

At this rapturous climax she woke to find the air full of music, and to see Helen standing tall and white in the moonlight that streamed in at the open window.

"Hush, hide behind the curtains and listen; it's a serenade," whispered Helen, as Amy stole to her side.

Shrouded in the drapery, they leaned and listened till the song ended, then Amy peeped. A dark group stood below; all were bareheaded, and now seemed whispering together. Presently a single voice rose, singing an exquisite little French canzonet,[1] the refrain of which was a passionate repetition of the word *"Amie."* She thought she recognized the voice, and the sound of her own name uttered in such ardent tones made her heart beat and her color rise, for it seemed to signify that the serenade was for them. As the last melodious murmur ceased, there came a stifled laugh from below, and something fell into the balcony. Neither dared stir till the sound of departing feet reassured them; then creeping forward, Amy drew in a lovely bouquet of myrtle, roses, and great German for-get-me-nots, tied with a white ribbon and addressed in a dashing hand to *La belle Helene.*

"Upon my life, the romance has begun in earnest," laughed Helen, as she examined the flowers. "You are serenaded by some unknown nightingale, and I have

1. Lyric song.

flowers tossed up to me in the charming old style. Of course it is the baron, Amy."

"I hope so; but whoever it is, they are regular troubadours, and I'm delighted. I know the gloves will bring us fun of some kind. Do you take one and I'll take the other, and see who will find the baron first. Isn't it odd that they knew our names?"

"Amy, the writing on this card is very like that in the big book. I may be bewitched by this mid-summer moonlight, but it really is very like it. Come and see."

The two charming heads bent over the card, looking all the more charming for the disheveled curls and braids that hung about them as the girls laughed and whispered together in the softly brilliant light that filled the room.

"You are right; it is the same. The men who stared so at dinner are light-hearted students perhaps, and ready for any prank. Don't tell uncle, but let us see what will come of it. I begin to enjoy myself heartily now—don't you?" said Amy, laying her glove carefully away.

"I enjoyed myself before, but I think '*La belle Helene*' gives an added relish to life, *Amie*," laughed *Nell*, putting her flowers in water; and then both went back to their pillows, to dream delightfully till morning.

II
Karl, The Courier

"Three days, at least, before we reach Baden. How tiresome it is that uncle won't go faster!" said Amy, as she tied on her hat the next morning, wondering as she did so if the baron would take the same boat.

"As adventures have begun, I feel assured that they will continue to cheer the way; so resign yourself and be ready for anything," replied Helen, carefully arranging her bouquet in her traveling-basket.

A tap at the door, which stood half open, made both look up. A tall, brown, gentlemanly man, in a gray suit, with a leather bag slung over his shoulder, stood there, hat in hand, and meeting Helen's eyes, bowed respectfully, saying in good English, but with a strong German accent—

"Ladies, the major desired me to tell you the carriage waits."

"Why, who—" began Amy, staring with her blue eyes full of wonder at the stranger.

He bowed again, and said, simply—

"Karl Hoffman, at your service, mademoiselle."

"The courier—oh, yes! I forgot all about it. Please take these things."

Amy began to hand him her miscellaneous collection of bags, books, shawls and cushions.

"I'd no idea couriers were such decent creatures," whispered Amy, as they followed him along the hall.

"Don't you remember the raptures Mrs. Mortimer used to have over their Italian courier, and her funny description of him? 'Beautiful to behold, with a night of hair, eyes full of an infinite tenderness, and a sumptuous cheek.'"

Both girls laughed, and Amy averred that Karl's eyes danced with merriment as he glanced over his shoulder, as the silvery peal sounded behind him.

"Hush! He understands English; we must be careful," said Helen, and neither spoke again till they reached the carriage.

Everything was ready, and as they drove away, the major, leaning luxuriously back, exclaimed—

"Now I begin to enjoy traveling, for I'm no longer worried by the thought of luggage, time-tables, trains, and the everlasting perplexity of thalers, kreutzers, and pfenninges.[2] This man is a treasure; everything is done in the best manner, and his knowledge of matters is really amazing."

2 German money.

THE BARON'S GLOVES

"He's a very gentlemanly-looking person," said Amy, eyeing a decidedly aristocratic foot through the front window of the carriage, for Karl sat up beside the driver.

"He *is* a gentleman, my dear. Many of these couriers are well born and educated, but, being poor, prefer this business to any other, as it gives them variety, and often pleasant society. I've had a long talk with Hoffman, and find him an excellent and accomplished fellow. He has lost his fortune, it seems, through no fault of his own, so being fond of a roving life, turned courier for a time, and we are fortunate to have secured him."

"But one doesn't know how to treat him," said Helen. "I don't like to address him as a servant, and yet it's not pleasant to order a gentleman about."

"Oh, it will be easy enough as we go on together. Just call him Hoffman, and behave as if you knew nothing about his past. He begged me not to mention it, but I thought you'd like the romance of the thing. Only don't either of you run away with him, as Ponsonby's daughter did with her courier, who wasn't a gentleman, by the way."

"Not handsome enough," said Amy. "I don't like blue eyes and black hair. His manners are nice, but he looks like a gypsy, with his brown face and black beard: doesn't he, Nell?"

18

"Not at all. Gypsies haven't that style of face; they are thin, sharp, and clever in feature as in nature. Hoffman has large, well-molded features, and a mild, manly expression, which gives one confidence in him."

"He has a keen, wicked look in his blue eyes, as you will see, Nell. I mean mischievously, not malignantly wicked. He likes fun, I'm sure, for he laughed about the 'sumptuous cheek' till his own were red, though he dared not show it, and was as grave as an owl when we met uncle," said Amy, smiling at the recollection.

"We shall go by boat to Biebrich, and then by rail to Heidelberg. We shall get in late tomorrow night, but can rest a day, and then on to Baden. Here we are; now make yourselves easy, as I do, and let Karl take care of everything."

And putting his hands in his pockets, the major strolled about the boat, while the courier made matters comfortable for the day. So easily and well did he do his duty that both girls enjoyed watching him after he had established them on the shady side of the boat, with campstools for their feet, cushions to lean on, books and bags laid commodiously at hand.

As they sailed up the lovely Rhine they grew more and more enthusiastic in their admiration and curiosity, and finding the meager description of the guide-books very unsatisfactory, Amy begged her uncle to tell her all the legends of picturesque ruin, rock and river, as they passed.

"Bless me, child, I know nothing; but here's Hoffman, a German born, who will tell you everything, I dare say. Karl, what's that old castle up there? The young ladies want to know about it."

Leaning on the railing, Hoffman told the story so well that he was kept explaining and describing for an hour, and when he went away to order lunch, Amy declared it was as pleasant as reading fairy tales to listen to his dramatic histories and legends.

At lunch the major was charmed to find his favorite wines and dishes without any need of consulting dictionary or phrase-book beforehand, or losing his temper in vain attempts to make himself understood.

On reaching Biebrich, tired and hungry, at nightfall, everything was ready for them, and all went to bed praising Karl, the courier, though Amy, with unusual prudence, added—

"He is a new broom now; let us wait a little before we judge."

All went well next day till nightfall, when a most untoward accident occurred, and Helen's adventures began in earnest. The three occupied a private railway car, and being weary with long sitting, Helen got out at one of the stations where the train paused for ten minutes. A rosy sunset tempted her to the end of the platform, and there she found, what nearly all foreign railway stations possess, a charming little garden.

Amy was very tired, rather cross, and passionately fond of flowers, so when an old woman offered to pull a nosegay for "the gracious lady," Helen gladly waited for it, hoping to please the invalid. Twice the whistle warned her, and at last she ran back, but only in time to see the train move away, with her uncle gesticulating wildly to the guard, who shook his stupid German head, and refused to see the dismayed young lady imploring him to wait for her.

Just as the train was vanishing from the station, a man leaped from a second-class carriage at the risk of his neck, and hurried back to find Helen looking pale and bewildered, as well she might, left alone and money-less at night in a strange town.

"Mademoiselle, it is I; rest easy; and we can soon go on; a train passes in two hours, and we can telegraph to Heidelberg that they may not fear for you."

"Oh, Hoffman, how kind of you to stop for me!

What should I have done without you, for uncle takes care of all the money, and I have only my watch."

Helen's usual self-possession rather failed her in the flurry of the moment, and she caught Karl's arm with a feminine little gesture of confidence very pleasant to see. Leading her to the waiting-room, he ordered supper, and put her into the care of the woman of the place, while he went to make inquiries and dispatch the telegram. In half an hour he returned, finding Helen refreshed and cheerful, though a trace of anxiety was still visible in her watchful eyes.

"All goes excellently, mademoiselle. I have sent word to several posts along the road that we are coming by the night train, so that Monsieur le Major will rest tranquil till we meet. It is best that I give you some money, lest such a mishap should again occur; it is not likely so soon; nevertheless, here is both gold and silver. With this, one can make one's way everywhere. Now, if mademoiselle will permit me to advise, she will rest for an hour, as we must travel till dawn. I will keep guard without and watch for the train."

He left her, and having made herself comfortable on one of the sofas, she lay watching the tall shadow pass and repass door and window, as Karl marched up and down the platform, with the tireless tramp of a sentinel on duty. A pleasant sense of security stole over her, and with a smile at Amy's enjoyment of the adventure when it was over, Helen fell asleep.

A far-off shriek half woke her, and starting up, she turned to meet the courier coming in to wake her. Up thundered the train, every carriage apparently full of sleepy passengers, and the guard in a state of sullen wrath at some delay, the consequences of which would fall heaviest on him.

From carriage to carriage hurried Karl and his charge, to be met with everywhere by the cry, "All full," in many languages, and with every aspect of inhospitality. One carriage only showed two places; the other seats were occupied by six students, who gallantly invited the lady to enter. But Helen shrunk back, saying—

"Is there no other place?"

"None, mademoiselle; this, or remain till morning," said Karl.

"Where will you go if I take this place?"

"Among the luggage—anywhere; it is nothing. But we must decide at once."

"Come with me; I'm afraid to be locked in here alone," said Helen, desperately.

"Mademoiselle forgets I am her courier."

"I do not forget that you are a gentleman. Pray come in; my uncle will thank you."

"I will," and with a sudden brightening of the eyes, a grateful glance, and an air of redoubled respect, Hoffman followed her into the carriage.

They were off at once, and the thing was done before Helen had time to feel anything but the relief which the protection of his presence afforded her.

The young gentlemen stared at the veiled lady and her grim escort, joked under their breath, and looked wistfully at the suppressed cigars, but behaved with exemplary politeness till sleep overpowered them, and one after the other dropped off asleep to dream of their respective Gretchens.

Helen could not sleep, and for hours sat studying the unconscious faces before her, the dim landscape flying past the windows, or forgot herself in reveries.

Hoffman remained motionless and silent, except when she addressed him, wakeful also, and assiduous in making the long night as easy as possible.

It was past midnight, and Helen's heavy eyelids were beginning to droop, when suddenly there came and awful crash, a pang of mortal fear, then utter oblivion.

LOUISA MAY ALCOTT

As her senses returned she found herself lying in a painful position under what had been the roof of the car; something heavy weighed down her lower limbs, and her dizzy brain rung with a wild uproar of shrieks and groans, eager voices, the crash of wood and iron, and the shrill whistle of the engine, as it rushed away for help.

Through the darkness she heard the pant as of someone struggling desperately, then a cry close by her, followed by a strong voice exclaiming, in an agony of suspense—

"My God, will no one come!"

"Hoffman, are you there?" cried Helen, groping in the gloom, with a thrill of joy at the sound of a familiar voice.

"Thank heaven, you are safe. Lie still. I will save you. Help is coming. Have no fear!" panted the voice, with an undertone of fervent gratitude in its breathless accents.

"What has happened? Where are the rest?"

"We have been thrown down an embankment. The lads are gone for help. God only knows what harm is done."

Karl's voice died in a stifled groan, and Helen cried out in alarm—

"Where are you? You are hurt?"

"Not much. I keep the ruins from falling in to crush us. Be quiet, they are coming."

A shout answered the faint halloo he gave as if to guide them to the spot, and a moment after, five of the students were swarming about the wreck, intent on saving the three whose lives were still in danger.

A lamp torn from some demolished carriage was held through an opening, and Helen saw a sight that made her blood chill in her veins. Across her feet, crushed and bleeding, lay the youngest of the students, and kneeling close beside him was Hoffman, supporting by main strength a mass of timber, which otherwise would fall and crush them all. His face was ghastly pale, his eyes haggard with pain and suspense, and great drops stood upon his forehead. But as she looked, he smiled with a cheery—

"Bear up, dear lady, we shall soon be out of danger. Now, lads, work with a will; my strength is going fast."

They did work like heroes, and even in her pain and peril, Helen admired the skill, energy, and courage of the young men, who, an hour ago, had seemed to have no ideas above pipes and beer. Soon Hoffman was free, the poor senseless youth lifted out, and then, as tenderly as if she were a child, they raised and set her down, faint but unhurt, in a wide meadow, already strewn with sad tokens of the wreck.

Karl was taken possession of as well as herself, forced to rest a moment, drink a cordial draught from someone's flask, and be praised, embraced, and enthusiastically blessed by the impetuous youths.

"Where is the boy who was hurt? Bring him to me. I am strong now. I want to help. I have salts in my pocket, and I can bind up his wounds," said Helen, soon herself again.

Karl and Helen soon brought back life and sense to the boy, and never had a human face looked so lovely as did Helen's to the anxious comrades when she looked up in the moonlight with a joyful smile, and softly whispered—

"He is alive."

For an hour terrible confusion reigned; then the panic subsided a little, and such of the carriages as were whole were made ready to carry away as many as possible; the rest must wait till a return train could be sent for them.

A struggle of course ensued, for everyone wished to go on, and fear made many selfish. The wounded, the women and children, were taken, as far as possible, and the laden train moved away, leaving many anxious watchers behind.

Helen had refused to go, and had given her place to poor Conrad, thereby overwhelming his brother and comrades with gratitude. Two went on with the wounded lad; the rest remained, and chivalrously devoted themselves to Helen as a body-guard.

The moon shone clearly, the wide field was miles from any hamlet, and a desolate silence succeeded to the late uproar, as the band of waiters roamed about, longing for help and dawn.

"Mademoiselle, you shiver; the dew falls, and it is damp here; we must have a fire;" and Karl was away to a neighboring hedge, intent on warming his delicate charge if he felled a forest to do it.

The students rushed after him, and soon returned in triumph to build a glorious fire, which drew all forlorn wanderers to its hospitable circle. A motley assemblage; but mutual danger and discomfort produced mutual sympathy and good will, and a general atmosphere of friendship pervaded the party.

"Where is the brave Hoffman?" asked Wilhelm, the blonde student, who, being in the romantic period of youth, was already madly in love with Helen, and sat at her feet catching cold in the most romantic manner.

"Behold me! The little ones cry for hunger, so I ransack the ruins and bring away my spoils. Eat, Kinder,[3] eat and be patient."

As he spoke Karl appeared with an odd collection of

baskets, bags, and bottles, and with a fatherly air that won all the mothers, he gave the children whatever first appeared, making them laugh in spite of weariness and hunger by the merry speeches which accompanied his gifts.

"Youth too needs something. Here is your own basket with the lunch I ordered you. In a sad state of confusion, but still eatable. See, it is not bad," and he deftly spread on a napkin before Helen cold chicken, sandwiches, and fruit.

His care for the little ones as well as for herself touched her and her eyes filled, as she remembered that she owed her life to him, and recalled the sight of his face in the overturned car.

Her voice trembled a little as she thanked him, and the moonlight betrayed her wet eyes. He fancied she was worn out with excitement and fatigue, and anxious to cheer her spirits, he whispered to Wilhelm and his mates—

"Singing, then, comrades, and while away this tedious night. It is hard for all to wait so long, and the babies need a lullaby."

The young men laughed and sang as only German students can sing, making the night musical with blithe drinking songs, tender love-lays, battle-hymns, and Volkslieder sweeter than any songs across the water.

Every heart was cheered and warmed by the magic

of the music, the babies fell asleep, strangers grew friendly, fear changed to courage, and the most forlorn felt the romance of that bivouac under the summer sky.

Dawn was reddening the east when a welcome whistle broke up the camp. Everyone hurried to the railway, but Helen paused to gather a handful of blue forget-me-nots, saying to Hoffman, who waited with her wraps on his arm—

"It has been a happy night, in spite of the danger and discomfort. I shall not soon forget it; and take these as a souvenir."

He smiled, standing bare-headed in the chilly wind, for his hat was lost, his coat torn, hair disheveled, and one hand carelessly bound up in his handkerchief. Helen saw these marks of the night's labors and perils for the first time, and as soon as they were seated desired to see his hand.

"It is nothing—a scratch, a mere scratch, I give you my word, mademoiselle," he began, but Wilhelm unceremoniously removed the handkerchief, showing a torn and bleeding hand which must have been exquisitely painful.

Helen turned pale, and with a reproachful glance skillfully bound it up again, saying, as she handed a silken scarf to Wilhelm—

"Make of that a sling, please, and put the poor hand in it. Care must be taken, or harm will come of it."

Hoffman submitted in bashful silence, as if surprised and touched by the young lady's interest. She saw that, and added gratefully—

"I do not forget that you saved my life, though you seem to have done so. My uncle will thank you better than I can."

"I already have my reward, mademoiselle," he returned, with a respectful inclination and a look she could neither understand nor forget.

III

Amy's Adventure

The excitement and suspense of the major and Amy can be imagined when news of the accident reached them. Their gratitude and relief were intense when Helen appeared next morning, with the faithful Hoffman still at his post, though no longer able to disguise the fact that he was suffering from his wound.

When the story had been told, Karl was put under the surgeon's care, and all remained at Heidelberg for several days to rest and recover.

On the afternoon of the last day the major and young ladies drove off to the castle for a farewell view. Helen began to sketch the great stone lion's head above the grand terrace, the major smoked and chatted with a party of English artists whom he had met, and Amy, with a little lad for a guide, explored the old castle to her heart's content.

The sun set, and twilight began to fall when Helen put up her pencils, and the major set off to find Amy, who had been appearing and disappearing in every nook and cranny of the half-ruined castle.

Nowhere could he find her, and no voice answered when he called. The other visitors were gone, and the place seemed deserted, except by themselves and the old man who showed the ruins.

Becoming alarmed lest the girl had fallen somewhere, or lost her way among the vaults where the famous Tun[4] lies, the major called out old Hans with his lantern, and searched high and low.

Amy's hat, full of flowers and ferns, was found in the Lady's Walk, as the little terrace is called, but no other trace appeared, and Helen hurried to and fro in great distress, fearing all manner of dangers.

Meanwhile Amy, having explored every other part of the castle, went to take another look at the Tun, the dwarf, and the vaults.

Now little Anderl, her guide, had a great fear of ghosts, and legions were said to haunt the ruins after nightfall, so when Amy rambled on deeper and deeper into the gloom, the boy's courage ebbed away with every step; yet he was ashamed to own his fear, seeing that she had none.

Amy wanted to see a certain cell, where a nun was said to have pined to death because she would not listen to the Margraf's[5] love. The legend pleased the romantic

4. Large cask for holding wine.
5. Member of the German Nobility.   33

girl, and forgetful of waning daylight, gathering damps, and Anderl's reluctant service, she ran on, up steps and down, delighted with little arched doors, rusty chains on the walls, glimpses of sky through shattered roofs, and all manner of mysterious nooks and corners. Coming at last to a narrow cell, with a stone table, and heavy bolts on the old door, she felt sure this was poor Elfrida's prison, and called Anderl to come on with his candle, for the boy had lighted one, for his own comfort rather than hers. Her call was unanswered, and glancing back, she saw the candle placed on the ground, but no Anderl.

"Little coward; he has run away," she said, laughing; and having satisfied her curiosity, turned to retrace her steps—no easy task to one ignorant of the way, for vault after vault opened on both sides, and no path was discernible. In vain she tried to recall some landmark; the gloom had deepened and nothing was clear. On she hurried, but found no opening, and really frightened, stopped at last, calling the boy in a voice that woke a hundred echoes. But Anderl had fled home, thinking the lady would find her way back, and preferring to lose his kreutzers to seeing a ghost.

Poor Amy's bewilderment and alarm increased with every moment's delay, and hoping to come out somewhere, she ran on till a misstep jostled the candle from her hand and extinguished it.

Left in the dark, her courage deserted her, and she screamed desperately, like a lost child, and was fast getting into a state of frantic terror, when the sound of an approaching step reassured her.

Holding her breath, she heard a quick tread drawing nearer, as if guided by her cries, and, straining her eyes, she caught the outline of a man's figure in the gloom.

A sensation of intense joy rushed over her, and she was about to spring forward, when she remembered that as she could speak no German how could she explain her plight to the stranger, if he understood neither French nor English?

Fear took possession of her at the thought of meeting some rough peasant, or some rollicking student, to whom she could make no intelligible appeal or explanation.

Crouching close against the wall, she stood mute till the figure was very near. She was in the shadow of an angle, and the man paused, as if looking for the person who called for help.

"Who is lost here?" said a clear voice, in German.

Amy shrunk closer to the wall, fearing to speak, for the voice was that of a young man, and a low laugh followed the words, as if the speaker found the situation amusing.

"Mortal, ghost or devil, I'll find it," exclaimed the voice, and stepping forward, a hand groped for and found her.

"Lottchen, is it thou? Little rogue, thou shalt pay dearly for leading me on such a chase."

As he spoke he drew the girl toward him, but with a faint cry, a vain effort to escape, Amy's terror reached its climax, and spent with fatigue and excitement, she lost consciousness.

"Who the deuce is it, then? Lottchen never faints on a frolic. Some poor little girl lost in earnest. I must get her out of this gloomy place at once, and find her party afterward."

Lifting the slight figure in his arms, the young man hurried on, and soon came out through a shattered gateway into the shrubbery which surrounds the base of the castle.

Laying her on the grass, he gently chafed her hands, eyeing the pale, pretty face meantime with the utmost solicitude.

At his first glimpse of it he had started, smiled and made a gesture of pleasure and surprise, then gave himself entirely to the task of recovering the poor girl whom he had frightened out of her senses.

Very soon she looked up with dizzy eyes, and clasping her hands imploringly, cried, in English, like a bewildered child—

"I am lost! Oh, take me to my uncle."

"I will, the moment you can walk. Upon my soul, I meant to help you when I followed; but as you did not answer, I fancied it was Lottchen, the keeper's little girl. Pardon the fright I've caused you, and let me take you to your friends."

The true English accent of the words, and the hearty tone of sincerity in the apology, reassured Amy at once, and, rising, she said, with a faint smile and a petulant tone—

"I was very silly, but my guide ran away, my candle went out, I lost the path, and can speak no German; so I was afraid to answer you at first; and then I lost my wits altogether, for it's rather startling to be clutched in the dark, sir."

"Indeed it is. I was very thoughtless, but now let me atone for it. Where is your uncle, Miss Erskine?" asked the stranger, with respectful earnestness.

"You know my name?" cried Amy in her impulsive way.

"I have that happiness," was the answer, with a smile.

"But I don't know *you*, sir;" and she peered at him, trying to see his face in the darkness, for the copse was thick, and twilight had come on rapidly.

"Not yet; I live in hope. Shall we go? Your uncle will be uneasy."

"Where are we?" asked Amy, glad to move on, for the interview was becoming too personal even for her, and the stranger's manner fluttered her, though she enjoyed the romance of the adventure immensely.

"We are in the park which surrounds the castle. You were near the entrance to it from the vaults when you fainted."

"I wish I had kept on a little longer, and not disgraced myself by such a panic."

"Nay; that is a cruel wish, for then I should have lost the happiness of helping you."

They had been walking side by side, but were forced to pause on reaching a broken flight of steps, for Amy could not see the way before her.

"Let me lead you; it is steep and dark, but better than going a long way round through the dew," he said, offering his hand.

"Must we return by these dreadful vaults?" faltered Amy, shrinking back.

"It is the shortest and safest route, I assure you."

"Are you sure you know the way?"

"Quite sure. I have lived here by the week together. Do you fear to trust me?"

"No; but it is so dark, and everything is so strange to me. Can we get down safely? I see nothing but a black pit."

And Amy still hesitated, with an odd mixture of fear and coquetry.

"I brought you up in safety; shall I take you down again?" asked the stranger, with a smile flickering over his face.

Amy felt rather than saw it, and assuming an air of dignified displeasure, motioned him to proceed, which he did for three steps; then Amy slipped, and gladly caught at the arm extended to save her.

Without a word he took her hand and led her back through the labyrinth she had threaded in her bewilderment. A dim light filled the place, but with unerring steps her guide went on till they emerged into the courtyard.

Major Erskine's voice was audible, giving directions to the keeper, and Helen's figure visible as she groped among the shadows of the ruined chapel for her cousin.

"There are my friends. Now I am safe. Come and let

them thank you," cried Amy, in her frank, childlike warmth of manner.

"I want no thanks—forgive me—adieu," and hastily kissing the little hand that had lain so confidingly in his, the stranger was gone.

Amy rushed at once to Helen, and when the lost lamb had been welcomed, chidden, and exulted over, they drove home, listening to the very brief account that Amy gave of her adventure.

"Naughty little gad-about, how could you go and terrify me so, wandering in vaults with mysterious strangers, like the Countess of Rudolstadt. You are as wet and dirty as if you had been digging a well, yet you look as if you liked it," said Helen, as she led Amy into their room at the hotel.

"I do," was the decided answer, as the girl pulled a handkerchief off her head, and began to examine the corners of it. Suddenly she uttered a cry and flew to the light, exclaiming—

"Nell, Nell, look here! The same letters, 'S.P.,' the same coat of arms, the same perfume—it was the baron!"

"What? Who? Are you out of your mind?" said Helen, examining the large, fine cambric handkerchief, with its delicately stamped initials under the stag's head, and three stars on a heart-shaped shield. "Where did you get it?" she added, as she inhaled the soft odor of violets shaken from its folds.

Amy blushed and answered shyly, "I didn't tell you all that happened before uncle, but now I will. My hat was left behind, and when I recovered my wits after my fright, I found this tied over my head. Oh, Nell, it was very charming there in that romantic old park, and going through the vaults with him, and having my hand kissed at parting. No one ever did that before, and I like it."

Amy glanced at her hand as she spoke, and stood staring as if struck dumb, for there on her forefinger shone a ring she had never seen before.

"Look! Look! Mine is gone, and this in its place! Oh, Nell, what shall I do?" she said, looking half frightened, half pleased.

Helen examined the ring and shook her head, for it was far more valuable than the little pearl one that it replaced. Two tiny hands of finest gold were linked together about a diamond of great brilliancy; and on the inside appeared again the initials, "S.P."

"How did it happen?" she asked rather sternly.

"Upon my word, I don't know, unless he put it on while I was stupidly fainting. Rude man, to take advantage of me so. But, Nell, it is splendid, and what *shall* I do about it?"

"Tell uncle to find out the man and send back his things. It really is absurd, the manner in which German boys behave," and Helen frowned, though she was strongly tempted to laugh at the whole thing.

"He was neither a German nor a boy, but an English gentleman, I'm sure," began Amy rather offended.

"But 'S.P.' is a baron, you know, unless there are two Richmonds in the field," broke in Helen.

"I forgot that; never mind, it deepens the mystery; and after this performance, I'm prepared for any enormity. It's my fate; I submit," said Amy, tragically, as she waved her hand to and fro, pleased with the flash of the ring.

"Amy, I think on the whole I won't speak to uncle. He is quick to take offence, especially where we are concerned. He doesn't understand foreign ways, and may get into trouble. We will manage it quietly ourselves."

"How, Nell?"

"Karl is discreet; we will merely say we found these things and wish to discover the owner. He may know this 'S.P.' and, having learned his address, we can send them back. The man will understand; and as we leave tomorrow, we shall be out of the way before he can play any new prank."

"Have in Karl at once, for if I wear this lovely thing long I shall not be able to let it go at all. How dared the creature take such a liberty!" and Amy pulled off the ring with an expression of great scorn.

"Come into the salon and see what Karl says to the matter. Let me speak, or you will say too much. One must be prudent before—"

She was going to say "servants," but checked herself, and substituted "strangers," remembering gratefully how much she owed this man.

Hoffman came, looking pale, and with his hand in a sling, but was as gravely devoted as ever, and listened to Helen's brief story with serious attention.

"I will inquire, mademoiselle, and let you know at once. It is easy to find persons if one has a clue. May I see the handkerchief?"

Helen showed it. He glanced at the initials, and laid it down with a slight smile.

"The coat-of-arms is English, mademoiselle."

"Are you sure?"

"Quite so; I understand heraldry."

"But the initials stand for Sigismund Palsdorf, and

we know he is a German baron," broke in Amy, forgetting prudence in eagerness.

"If mademoiselle knows the name and title of this gentleman it will not be hard to find him."

"We only fancy it is the same because of the initials. I dare say it is a mistake, and the man is English. Inquire quietly, Hoffman, if you please, as this ring is of value, and I wish to restore it to its owner," said Helen, rather sharply.

"I shall do so, mademoiselle," and with his gentlemanly bow, the courier left the room.

"Bless me, what's that?" cried Amy, a moment afterward, as a ringing laugh echoed through the corridor— a laugh so full of hearty and infectious merriment that both girls smiled involuntarily, and Amy peeped out to see who the blithe personage might be.

An old gentleman was entering his room near by, and Karl was just about to descend the stairs. Both looked back at the girlish face peeping at them, but both were quite grave, and the peal of laughter remained a mystery, like all the rest of it.

Late in the evening Hoffman returned to report that a party of young Englishmen had visited the castle that afternoon, and had left by the evening train. One of them had been named Samuel Peters, and he, doubtless, was the owner of the ring.

A humorous expression lurked in the courier's eye as he made his report, and heard Amy exclaim, in a tone of disgust and comical despair—

"Samuel Peters! That spoils all the romance and dims the beauty of the diamond. To think that a Peters should be a hero to whom I owe my safety, and a Samuel should leave me this token of regard!"

"Hush, Amy," whispered Helen. "Thanks, Hoffman; we must wait now for chance to help us."

IV

A Polish Exile

"Room for one here, sir," said the guard, as the train stopped at Carlsruhe the next day, on its way from Heidelberg to Baden.

The major put down his guide-book, Amy opened her eyes, and Helen removed her shawl from the opposite seat, as a young man, wrapped in a cloak, with a green shade over his eyes, and a general air of feebleness, got in and sank back with a sigh of weariness or pain. Evidently an invalid, for his face was thin and pale, his dark hair cropped short, and the ungloved hand attenuated and delicate as a woman's. A sidelong glance from under the deep shade seemed to satisfy him regarding his neighbors, and drawing his cloak about him with a slight shiver, he leaned into the corner and seemed to forget that he was not alone.

Helen and Amy exchanged glances of compassionate interest, for women always pity invalids, especially if young, comely and of the opposite sex. The major took one look, shrugged his shoulders, and returned to his book.

Presently a hollow cough gave Helen a pretext for discovering the nationality of the newcomer.

"Do the open windows inconvenience you, sir?" she asked in English.

No answer; the question evidently unintelligible.

She repeated it in French, lightly touching his cloak to arrest his attention.

Instantly a smile broke over the handsome mouth, and in the purest French he assured her that the fresh air was most agreeable, and begged pardon for annoying them with his troublesome cough.

"Not an invalid, I hope, sir?" said the major, in his bluff yet kindly voice.

"They tell me I can have no other fate; that my malady is fatal; but I still hope and fight for my life; it is all I have to give my country now."

A stifled sigh and a sad emphasis on the last word roused the sympathy of the girls, the interest of the major.

He took another survey, and said, with a tone of satisfaction, as he marked the martial carriage of the young man, and caught a fiery glance of the half-hidden eyes—

"You are a soldier, sir?"

"I was; I am nothing now but an exile, for Poland is in chains."

THE BARON'S GLOVES

The words "Poland" and "exile" brought up all the pathetic stories of that unhappy country which the three listeners had ever heard, and won their interest at once.

"You were in the late revolution, perhaps?" asked the major, giving the unhappy outbreak the most respectful name he could use.

"From beginning to end."

"Oh, tell us about it; we felt much sympathy for you, and longed to have you win," cried Amy, with such genuine interest and pity in her tone, it was impossible to resist.

Pressing both hands upon his breast, the young man bent low, with a flush of feeling on his pale cheek, and answered eagerly—

"Ah, you are kind; it is balm to my sore heart to hear words like these. I thank you, and tell you what you will. It is but little that I do, yet I give my life, and die a long death, instead of a quick, brave one with my comrades."

"You are young to have borne a part in a revolution, sir," said the major, who pricked up his ears like an old war-horse at the sound of battle.

"My friends and myself left the University at Varsovie, as volunteers; we did our part, and now all lie in their graves but three."

"You were wounded, it seems?"

"Many times. Exposure, privation, and sorrow will finish what the Russian bullets began. But it is well. I have no wish to see my country enslaved, and I can no longer help her."

"Let us hope that a happier future waits for you both. Poland loves liberty too well, and has suffered too much for it, to be kept long in captivity."

Helen spoke warmly, and the young man listened with a brightening face.

"It is a kind prophecy; I accept it, and take courage. God knows I need it," he added low to himself.

"Are you bound for Italy?" said the major, in a most un-English fit of curiosity.

"For Geneva first, Italy later, unless Montreaux is mild enough for me to winter in. I go to satisfy my friends, but doubt if it avails."

"Where is Montreaux?" asked Amy.

"Near Clarens, where Rousseau wrote his Heloise, and Vevay, where so many English go to enjoy Chillon. The climate is divine for unfortunates like myself, and life more cheap there than in Italy."

Here the train stopped again, and Hoffman came to ask if the ladies desired anything.

At the sound of his voice the young Pole started,

looked up, and exclaimed, with the vivacity of a foreigner, in German—

"By my life; it is Karl! Behold me, old friend, and satisfy me that it is thyself by a handshake."

"Casimer! What wind blows thee hither, my boy, in such sad plight?" replied Hoffman, grasping the slender hand outstretched to him.

"I fly from an enemy for the first time in my life, and, like all cowards, shall be conquered in the end. I wrote thee I was better, but the wound in the breast reopened, and nothing but a miracle will save me. I go to Switzerland; and thou?"

"Where my master commands. I serve this gentleman, now."

"Hard changes for both, but with health thou art king of circumstances, while I— Ah, well, the good God knows best. Karl, go thou and buy me two of those pretty baskets of grapes; I will please myself by giving them to these pitying angels. Speak they German?"

"One, the elder; but they understand not this rattle of ours."

Karl disappeared, and Helen, who had understood the rapid dialogue, tried to seem as unconscious as Amy.

"Say a friendly word to me at times; I am so homesick and faint-hearted, my Hoffman. Thanks; they are almost worthy the lips that shall taste them."

Taking the two little osier baskets, laden with yellow and purple clusters, Casimer offered them, with a charming mixture of timidity and grace, to the girls, saying, like a grateful boy—

"You give me kind words and good hopes; permit that I thank you in this poor way."

"I drink success to Poland," cried Helen, lifting a great, juicy grape to her lips, like a little purple goblet, hoping to hide her confusion under a playful air.

The grapes went round, and healths were drunk with much merriment, for in traveling on the Continent it is impossible for the gruffest, primmest person to long resist the frank courtesy and vivacious chat of foreigners.

The major was unusually social and inquisitive, and while the soldiers fought their battles over again, the girls listened and took notes, with feminine wits on the alert to catch any personal revelations which might fall from the interesting stranger. The wrongs and sufferings of Poland were discussed so eloquently that both young ladies were moved to declare the most undying hatred of Russia, Prussia, and Austria, the most intense sympathy for "poor Pologne." All day they traveled together, and as

Baden-Baden approached, they naturally fell to talking of the gay place.

"Uncle, I must try my fortune once. I've set my heart upon it, and so has Nell. We want to know how gamblers feel, and to taste the fascination of the game which draws people here from all parts of Europe," said Amy, in her half-pleading, half-imperious way.

"You may risk one napoleon each, as I foolishly promised you should, when I little thought you would ever have an opportunity to remind me of my promise. It's not an amusement for respectable Englishwomen, or men either. You will agree with me there, monsieur?" and the major glanced at the Pole, who replied, with his peculiar smile—

"Surely, yes. It is great folly and waste of time and money; yet I have known one man who found some good in it, or, rather, brought good out of it. I have a friend who has a mania for giving. His own fortune was spent in helping needy students at the University, and poor professors. This displeased his father, and he refused supplies, except enough for his simple personal wants. Sigismund chafed at this; and being skilful at all games, as a gentleman may be in the way of amusement, he resolved to play with those whose money was wasted on frivolities, and give his winnings to his band of paupers."

"How did it succeed, this odd fancy?" asked Helen, with an interested face, while Amy pinched her arm at the word "Sigismund."

"Excellently. My friend won often, and as his purpose became known it caused no unkind feeling, this unusual success, for fortune seemed to favor his kind object."

"Wrong, nevertheless, to do evil that good may come of it," said the major, morally.

"It may be so; but it is not for me to censure my benefactor. He has done much for my countrymen and me, and is truly noble. I can see no fault in him."

"What an odd name! Sigismund is German, is it not?" asked Amy, in the most artless tone of interest.

"Yes, mademoiselle, and Palsdorf is a true German; much courage, strength and intellect, with the gayety and simplicity of a boy. He hates slavery of all kinds, and will be free at all costs. He is a good son, but his father is tyrannical, and asks too much. Sigismund will not submit to sell himself, and so is in disgrace for a time."

"Palsdorf!—was not that the name of the count or baron we heard them talking of at Coblentz?" said Helen to Amy, with a well-feigned air of uncertainty.

"Yes; I heard something of a duel and a broken betrothal, I think. The people seemed to consider the baron a wild young man, so it could not have been your friend, sir," was Amy's reply, glancing at Helen with mirthful eyes, as if to say, "How our baron haunts us!"

"It is the same, doubtless. Many consider him wild, because he is original, and dares act for himself. As it is well known, I may tell you the truth of the duel and the betrothal, if you care to hear a little romance."

Casimer looked eager to defend his friend, and as the girls were longing to hear the romance, permission was given.

"In Germany, you know, the young people are often betrothed in childhood by the parents, and sometimes never meet till they are grown. Usually all goes well; but not always, for love cannot come at command. Sigismund was plighted, when a boy of fifteen, to his young cousin, and then sent away to the University till of age. On returning, he was to travel a year or two, and then marry. He gladly went away, and with increasing disquiet saw the time draw near when he must keep his troth-plight."

"Hum! Loved someone else. Very unfortunate, to be sure," said the major with a sigh.

"Not so; he only loved his liberty, and pretty Minna was less dear than a life of perfect freedom. He went back at the appointed time, saw his cousin, tried to do his duty and love her; found it impossible, and, discovering that Minna loved another, vowed he would never make her unhappiness as well as his own. The old baron stormed, but the young one was firm, and would not listen to a marriage without love; but pleaded for Minna, wished his rival success, and set out again on his travels."

"And the duel?" asked the major, who took less interest in love than war.

"That was as characteristic as the other act. A son of one high in office at Berlin circulated false reports of the cause of Palsdorf's refusal of the alliance—reports injurious to Minna. Sigismund settled the matter in the most effectual manner, by challenging and wounding the man. But for court influence it would have gone hardly with my friend. The storm, however, has blown over; Minna will be happy with her lover, and Sigismund with his liberty, till he tires of it."

"Is he handsome, this hero of yours?" said Amy, feeling the ring under her glove, for in spite of Helen's advice, she insisted on wearing it, that it might be at hand to return at any moment, should chance again bring the baron in their way.

"A true German of the old type; blond and blue-eyed, tall and strong. My hero in good truth—brave and loyal, tender and true," was the enthusiastic answer.

"I hate fair men," pouted Amy, under her breath, as the major asked some question about hotels.

"Take a new hero, then; nothing can be more romantic than that," whispered Helen, glancing at the pale, dark-haired figure wrapped in the military cloak opposite.

"I will, and leave the baron to you," said Amy, with a stifled laugh.

"Hush! Here are Baden and Karl," replied Helen, thankful for the interruption.

All was bustle in a moment, and taking leave of them with an air of reluctance, the Pole walked away, leaving Amy looking after him wistfully, quite unconscious that she stood in everybody's way, and that her uncle was beckoning impatiently from the carriage door.

"Poor boy! I wish he had someone to take care of him," she sighed, half aloud.

"Mademoiselle, the major waits;" and Karl came up, hat in hand, just in time to hear her and glance after Casimer, with an odd expression.

V
Ludmilla

"I wonder what that young man's name was. Did he mention it, Helen?" said the major, pausing in his march up and down the room, as if the question was suggested by the sight of the little baskets, which the girls had kept.

"No, uncle; but you can easily ask Hoffman," replied Helen.

"By the way, Karl, who was the Polish gentleman who came on with us?" asked the major a moment afterward, as the courier came in with newspapers.

"Casimer Teblinski, sir."

"A baron?" asked Amy, who was decidedly a young lady of one idea just then.

"No, mademoiselle, but of a noble family, as the 'ski' denotes, for that is to Polish and Russian names what 'von' is to German and 'de' to French."

"I was rather interested in him. Where did you pick him up, Hoffman?" said the major.

"In Paris, where he was with fellow-exiles."

"He is what he seems, is he?"—no impostor, or anything of that sort? One is often deceived, you know."

"On my honor, sir, he is a gentleman, and as brave as he is accomplished and excellent."

"Will he die?" asked Amy, pathetically.

"With care he would recover, I think; but there is no one to nurse him, so the poor lad must take his chance and trust in heaven for help."

"How sad! I wish we were going his way, so that we might do something for him—at least give him the society of his friends."

Helen glanced at Hoffman, feeling that if he were not already engaged by them, he would devote himself to the invalid without any thought of payment.

"Perhaps we are. You want to see the Lake of Geneva, Chillon, and that neighborhood. Why not go now instead of later?"

"Will you, uncle? That's capital! We need say nothing, but go on and help the poor boy, if we can."

Helen spoke like a matron of forty, and looked as full of maternal kindness as if the Pole were not out of his teens.

The courier bowed, the major laughed behind his paper, and Amy gave a sentimental sigh to the memory of the baron, in whom her interest was failing.

They only caught a glimpse of the Pole that evening

at the Kursaal, but next morning they met, and he was invited to join their party for a little expedition.

The major was in fine spirits, and Helen assumed her maternal air toward both invalids, for the sound of that hollow cough always brought a shadow over her face, recalling the brother she had lost.

Amy was particularly merry and charming, and kept the whole party laughing at her comical efforts to learn Polish and teach English as they drove up the mountainside to the old Schloss.

"I'm not equal to mounting all those steps for a view I've seen a dozen times; but pray take care of the child, Nell, or she'll get lost again, as at Heidelberg," said the major, when they had roamed about the lower part of the place; for a cool seat in the courtyard and a glass of beer were more tempting than turrets and prospects to the stout gentleman.

"She shall not be lost; I am her body-guard. It is steep—permit that I lead you, mademoiselle;" Casimer offered his hand to Amy, and they began their winding way. As she took the hand, the girl blushed and half smiled, remembering the vaults and the baron.

"I like this better," she said to herself, as they climbed step by step, often pausing to rest in the embrasures of the loopholes, where the sun glanced in, the balmy wind blew, and vines peeped from without, making a pretty picture of the girl, as she sat with rosy color on her usually pale cheeks, brown curls fluttering about her forehead, laughing lips, and bright eyes full of pleasant changes. Leaning opposite in the narrow stairway, Casimer had time to study the little tableau in many lights, and in spite of the dark glasses, to convey warm glances of admiration, of which, however, the young coquette seemed utterly unconscious.

Helen came leisurely after, and Hoffman followed with a telescope, wishing, as he went, that his countrywomen possessed such dainty feet as those going on before him, for which masculine iniquity he will be pardoned by all who have seen the foot of a German Fraulein.

It was worth the long ascent, that wide-spread landscape basking in the August glow.

Sitting on a fallen block of stone, while Casimer held a sun-umbrella over her, Amy had raptures at her ease; while Helen sketched and asked questions of Hoffman, who stood beside her, watching her progress with interest. Once when, after repeated efforts to catch a curious effect of light and shade, she uttered an impatient little exclamation, Karl made a gesture as if to take the pencil and show her, but seemed to recollect himself and drew back with a hasty "Pardon, mademoiselle." Helen glanced up and saw the expression of his face, which plainly betrayed that for a moment the gentleman had forgotten that he was a courier. She was glad of it, for it was a daily trial to her to order this man about; and following the womanly impulse, she smiled and offered the pencil, saying simply—

"I felt sure you understood it; please show me."

He did so, and a few masterly strokes gave the sketch what it needed. As he bent near her to do this, Helen stole a glance at the grave, dark face, and suddenly a disturbed look dawned in the eyes fixed on the glossy black locks pushed off the courier's forehead, for he had removed his hat when she spoke to him. He seemed to feel that something was amiss, shot a quick glance at her, returned the pencil and rose erect, with an almost defiant air, yet something of shame in his eye, as his lips moved as if to speak impetuously. But not a word did he utter, for Helen touched her forehead significantly, and said in a low tone—

"I am an artist; let me recommend Vandyke brown, which is not affected by heat."

Hoffman looked over his shoulder at the other pair, but Amy was making an ivy wreath for her hat, and the Pole pulling sprays for the absorbing work. Speaking rapidly, Karl said, with a peculiar blending of merriment, humility, and anxiety in his tone—

"Mademoiselle, you are quick to discover my disguise; will you also be kind in concealing? I have enemies as well as friends, whom I desire to escape. I would earn my bread unknown; Monsieur le Major keeps my foolish secret; may I hope for equal goodness from yourself?"

"You may, I do not forget that I owe my life to you, nor that you are a gentleman. Trust me, I never will betray you."

"Thanks, thanks! There will come a time when I may confess the truth and be myself, but not yet," and his regretful tone was emphasized by an impatient gesture, as if concealment was irksome.

"Nell, come down to lunch; uncle is signaling as if he'd gone mad. No, monsieur, it is quite impossible; you cannot reach the harebells without risking too much; come away and forget that I wanted them."

Amy led the way, and all went down more quietly than they came up, especially Helen and Hoffman. An excellent lunch waited on one of the tables in front of the old gateway, and having done justice to it, the major made himself comfortable with a cigar, bidding the girls keep near, for they must be off in half an hour. Hoffman went to see to the horses, Casimer strolled away with him, and the young ladies went to gather wild flowers at the foot of the tower.

"Not a harebell here; isn't it provoking, when they grow in tufts up there, where one can't reach them. Mercy, what's that? Run, Nell, the old wall is coming down!"

Both had been grubbing in a damp nook, where ferns and mosses grew luxuriantly; the fall of a bit of stone and a rending sound above made them fly back to the path and look up.

Amy covered her eyes, and Helen grew pale, for part way down the crumbling tower, clinging like a bird to the thick ivy stems, hung Casimer, coolly gathering harebells from the clefts of the wall.

"Hush; don't cry out or speak; it may startle him. Crazy boy! Let us see what he will do," whispered Helen.

"He can't go back, the vines are so torn and weak; and how will he get down the lower wall? For you see the ivy grows up from that ledge, and there is nothing below. How could he do it? I was only joking when I lamented that there were no knights now, ready to leap into a lion's den for a lady's glove," returned Amy, half angry.

The Baron's Gloves

In breathless silence they watched the climber till his cap was full of flowers, and taking it between his teeth, he rapidly swung down to the wide ledge, from which there appeared to be no way of escape but a reckless leap of many feet on to the turf below.

The girls stood in the shadow of an old gateway, unperceived, and waited anxiously for what should follow.

Lightly folding and fastening the cap together, he dropped it down, and, leaning forward, tried to catch the top of a young birch rustling close by the wall. Twice he missed it; the first time he frowned, but the second he uttered an emphatic, "Deuce take it!"

Helen and Amy looked at each other with a mutual smile and exclamation—

"He knows some English, then!"

There was time for no more—violent rustle, a boyish laugh, and down swung the slender tree, with the young man clinging to the top.

As he landed safely, Helen cried, "Bravo!" and Amy rushed out, exclaiming reproachfully, yet admiringly—

"How could you do it and frighten us so? I shall never express a wish before you again, for if I wanted the moon you'd rashly try to get it, I know."

"*Certainement,* mademoiselle," was the smiling

reply. Casimer presented the flowers, as if the exploit was a mere trifle.

"Now I shall go and press them at once in uncle's guide-book. Come and help me, else you will be in mischief again." And Amy led the way to the major with her flowers and their giver.

Helen roamed into one of the ruined courts for a last look at a fountain which pleased her eye. A sort of cloister ran round the court, open on both sides, and standing in one of these arched nooks, she saw Hoffman and a young girl talking animatedly. The girl was pretty, well dressed, and seemed refusing something for which the other pleaded eagerly. His arm was about her, and she leaned affectionately upon him, with a white hand now and then caressing his face, which was full of sparkle and vivacity now. They seemed about to part as Helen looked, for the maiden standing on tiptoe, laughingly offered her blooming cheek, and as Karl kissed it warmly, he said in German, so audibly Helen heard every word—

"Farewell, my Ludmilla. Keep silent and I shall soon be with you. Embrace the little one, and do not let him forget me."

Both left the place as they spoke, each going a differ-

ent way, and Helen slowly returned to her party, saying
to herself in a troubled tone—

" 'Ludmilla' and 'the little one' are his wife and child,
doubtless. I wonder if uncle knows that."

When Hoffman next appeared she could not resist
looking at him; but the accustomed gravity was
resumed, and nothing remained of the glow and bright-
ness he had worn when with Ludmilla in the cloister.

VI

Chateau De La Tour

Helen looked serious and Amy indignant when their uncle joined them, ready to set out by the afternoon train, all having dined and rested after the morning's excursion.

"Well, little girls, what's the matter now?" he asked, paternally, for the excellent man adored his nieces.

"Helen says it's not best to go on with the Pole, and is perfectly nonsensical, uncle." Began Amy, petulantly, and not very coherently.

"Better be silly now than sorry by and by. I only suggested that, being interesting, and Amy romantic, she might find this young man too charming, if we see too much of him," said Helen.

"Bless my soul, what an idea!" cried the major. "Why, Nell, he's an invalid, a Catholic, and a foreigner, any one of which objections are enough to settle the matter. Little Amy isn't so foolish as to be in danger of losing her heart to a person so entirely out of the question as this poor lad, is she?"

"Of course not. *You* do me justice, uncle. Nell thinks

she may pity and pet anyone she likes because she is five years older than I, and entirely forgets that she is a great deal more attractive than a feeble thing like me. I should as soon think of losing my heart to Hoffman as to the Pole, even if he wasn't what he is. One may surely be kind to a dying man, without being accused of coquetry;" and Amy sobbed in the most heart-rending manner.

Helen comforted her by withdrawing all objections, and promising to leave the matter in the major's hands. But she shook her head privately when she saw the ill-disguised eagerness with which her cousin glanced up and down the platform after they were in the train, and she whispered to her uncle, unobserved—

"Leave future meetings to chance, and don't ask the Pole in, if you can help it."

"Nonsense, my dear. You are as particular as your aunt. The lad amuses me, and you can't deny you like to nurse sick heroes," was all the answer she got, as the major, with true masculine perversity, put his head out of the window and hailed Casimer as he was passing with a bow.

"Here, Teblinski, my good fellow, don't desert us. We've always a spare seat for you, if you haven't pleasanter quarters."

With a flush of pleasure the young man came up, but hesitated to accept the invitation till Helen seconded it with a smile of welcome.

Amy was in an injured mood, and, shrouded in a great blue veil, pensively reclined in her corner as if indifferent to everything about her. But soon the cloud passed, and she emerged in a radiant state of good humor, which lasted unbroken until the journey ended.

For two days they went on together, a very happy party, for the major called in Hoffman to see his friend and describe the places through which they passed. An arrangement very agreeable to all, as Karl was a favorite, and everyone missed him when away.

At Lausanne they waited while he crossed the lake to secure rooms at Vevay. On his return he reported that all the hotels and pensions were full, but that at La Tour he had secured rooms for a few weeks in a quaint old chateau on the banks of the lake.

"Count Severin is absent in Egypt, and the house-keeper has permission to let the apartments to transient visitors. The suite of rooms I speak of were engaged to a party who are detained by sickness—they are cheap, pleasant, and comfortable. A salon and four bedrooms. I engaged them all, thinking that Teblinski might like a room there till he finds lodgings at Montreaux. We can enter at once, and I am sure the ladies will approve of the picturesque place."

"Well done, Hoffman; off we go without delay, for I really long to rest my old bones in something like a home, after this long trip," said the major, who always kept his little troop in light marching order.

The sail across that loveliest of lakes prepared the new-comers to be charmed with all they saw; and when, entering the old stone gate, they were led into a large saloon, quaintly furnished and opening into a terrace-garden overhanging the water, with Chillon and the Alps in sight, Amy declared nothing could be more perfect, and Helen's face proved her satisfaction.

An English widow and two quiet old German professors on a vacation were the only inmates besides themselves and the buxom Swiss housekeeper and her maids.

It was late when the party arrived, and there was only time for a hasty survey of their rooms and a stroll in the garden before dinner.

The great chamber, with its shadowy bed, dark mirrors, ghostly wainscot-doors and narrow windows, had not been brightened for a long time by such a charming little apparition as Amy when she shook out her airy muslins, smoothed her curls, and assumed all manner of distracting devices for the captivation of mankind. Even Helen, though not much given to personal vanity, found herself putting flowers in her hair, and studying the effect of bracelets on her handsome arms, as if there were some especial need of looking her best on this occasion.

Both were certainly great ornaments to the drawing-room that evening, as the old professors agreed while they sat blinking at them like a pair of benign owls. Casimer surprised them by his skill in music, for, though forbidden to sing on account of his weak lungs, he played as if inspired. Amy hovered about him like a moth; the major cultivated the acquaintance of the plump widow; and Helen stood at the window, enjoying the lovely night and music, till something happened that destroyed her pleasure in both.

The window was open, and, leaning from it, she was watching the lake, when the sound of a heavy sigh caught her ear. There was no moon, but through the starlight she saw a man's figure among the shrubs below, sitting with bent head and hidden face in the forlorn attitude of one shut out from the music, light, and gayety that reigned within.

"It is Karl," she thought, and was about to speak, when, as if startled by some sound she did not hear, he rose and vanished in the gloom of the garden.

"Poor man! He thought of his wife and child, perhaps, sitting here alone while all the rest make merry, with no care for him. Uncle must see to this;" and Helen fell into a reverie till Amy came to propose retiring.

"I meant to have seen where all these doors led, but was so busy dressing I had no time, so must leave it for my amusement tomorrow. Uncle says it's a very Radcliffian place. How like an angel that man did play!" chattered Amy, and lulled herself to sleep by humming the last air Casimer had given them.

Helen could not sleep, for the lonely figure in the garden haunted her, and she wearied herself with conjectures about Hoffman and his mystery. Hour after hour rung from the cuckoo-clock in the hall, but still she lay awake, watching the curious shadows in the room, and exciting herself with recalling the tales of German goblins with which the courier had amused them the day before.

"It is close and musty here, with all this old tapestry and stuff about; I'll open the other window," she thought; and, noiselessly slipping from Amy's side, she threw on wrapper and slippers, lighted her candle and tried to unbolt the tall, diamond-paned lattice. It was rusty and would not yield, and, giving it up, she glanced about to see whence air could be admitted. There were four doors in the room, all low and arched, with clumsy locks and heavy handles. One opened into a closet, one into the passage; the third was locked, but the fourth opened easily, and, lifting her light, she peeped into a small octagon room, full of all manner of curiosities. What they were she had no time to see, for her startled eyes were riveted on an object that turned her faint and cold with terror.

A heavy table stood in the middle of the room, and seated at it, with some kind of weapon before him, was a man who looked over his shoulder, with a ghastly face half hidden by hair and beard, and fierce black eyes as full of malignant menace as was the clinched hand holding the pistol. One instant Helen looked, the next flung to the door, bolted it and dropped into a chair, trembling in every limb. The noise did not wake Amy, and a moment's thought showed Helen the wisdom of keeping her in ignorance of this affair. She knew the major was close by, and possessing much courage, she resolved to wait a little before rousing the house.

Hardly had she collected herself, when steps were heard moving softly in the octagon room. Her light had gone out as she closed the door, and sitting close by in the dark, she heard the sound of someone breathing as he listened at the key-hole. Then a careful hand tried the door, so noiselessly that no sleeper would have been awakened; and as if to guard against a second surprise, the unknown person drew two bolts across the door and stole away.

"Safe for a time; but I'll not pass another night under this roof, unless this is satisfactorily cleared up," thought Helen, now feeling more angry than frightened.

The last hour that struck was three, and soon the summer dawn reddened the sky. Dressing herself, Helen sat by Amy, a sleepless guard, till she woke, smiling and rosy as a child. Saying nothing of her last night's alarm, Helen went down to breakfast a little paler than usual, but otherwise unchanged. The major never liked to be disturbed till he had broken his fast, and the moment they rose from the table he exclaimed—

"Now, girls, come and see the mysteries of Udolpho."

"I'll say nothing, yet," thought Helen, feeling braver by daylight, yet troubled by her secret, for Hoffman might be a traitor, and this charming chateau a den of thieves. Such things had been, and she was in a mood to believe anything.

The upper story was a perfect museum of antique relics, very entertaining to examine. Having finished these, Hoffman, who acted as guide, led them into a little gloomy room containing a straw pallet, a stone table with a loaf and pitcher on it, and, kneeling before a crucifix, where the light from a single slit in the wall fell on him, was the figure of a monk. The waxen mask was lifelike, the attitude effective, and the cell excellently arranged. Amy cried out when she first saw it, but a second glance reassured her, and she patted the baldhead approvingly, as Karl Explained—

"Count Severin is an antiquarian, and amuses himself with things of this sort. In old times there really was a hermit here, and this is his effigy. Come down these narrow stairs, if you please, and see the rest of the mummery."

Down they went, and the instant Helen looked about her, she burst into a hysterical laugh, for there sat her ruffian, exactly as she saw him, glaring over his shoulder with threatening eyes, and one hand on the pistol. They all looked at her, for she was pale, and her merriment unnatural; so, feeling she had excited curiosity, she gratified it by narrating her night's adventure. Hoffman looked much concerned.

"Pardon, mademoiselle, the door should have been bolted on this side. It usually is, but that room being unused, it was forgotten. I remembered it, and having risen early, crept up to make sure that you did not come upon this ugly thing unexpectedly. But I was too late, it seems; you have suffered, to my sorrow."

"Dear Nell, and that was why I found you so pale and cold and quiet, sitting by me when I woke, guarding me faithfully as you promised you would. How brave and kind you were!"

"Villain! I should much like to fire your own pistols at you for this prank of yours."

And Casimer laughingly filliped the image on its absurdly aquiline nose.

"What in the name of common sense is this goblin here for?" demanded the major, testily.

"There is a legend that once the owner of the chateau amused himself by decoying travelers here, putting them to sleep in that room, and by various devices alluring them thither. Here, one step beyond the threshold of the door, was a trap, down which the unfortunates were precipitated to the dungeon at the bottom of the tower, there to die and be cast into the lake through a water-gate, still to be seen. Severin keeps this flattering likeness of the rascal, as he does the monk above, to amuse visitors by daylight, not at night, mademoiselle."

And Hoffman looked wrathfully at the image, as if he would much enjoy sending it down the trap.

"How ridiculous! I shall not go about this place alone for fear of lighting upon some horror of this sort. I've had enough; come away into the garden; it's full of roses, and we may have as many as we like."

As she spoke, Amy involuntarily put out her hand for Casimer to lead her down the steep stone steps, and he pressed the little hand with a tender look which caused it to be hastily withdrawn.

"Here are your roses. Pretty flower; I know its meaning in English, for it is the same with us. To give a bud to a lady is to confess the beginning of love, a half open one tells of its growth, and a full-blown one is to declare one's passion. Do you have that custom in your land, mademoiselle?"

He had gathered the three as he spoke, and held the bud separately while looking at his companion wistfully.

"No, we are not poetical, like your people, but it is a

pretty fancy," and Amy settled her bouquet with an absorbed expression, though inwardly wondering what he would do with his flowers.

He stood silent a moment, with a sudden flush sweeping across his face, then flung all three into the lake with a gesture that made the girl start, and muttered between his teeth:

"No, no; for me it is too late."

She affected not to hear, but making up a second bouquet, she gave it to him, with no touch of coquetry in compassionate eyes or gentle voice.

"Make your room bright with these. When one is ill nothing is so cheering as the sight of flowers."

Meantime the others had descended and gone their separate ways.

As Karl crossed the courtyard, a little child ran to meet him with outstretched arms and a shout of satisfaction. He caught it up and carried it away on his shoulder, like one used to caress and be caressed by children.

Helen, waiting at the door of the tower while the major dusted his coat, saw this, and said, suddenly, directing his attention to man and child—

"He seems fond of little people. I wonder if he has any of his own."

"Hoffman? No, my dear; he's not married; I asked him that when I engaged him."

"And he said he was not?"

"Yes; he's not more than five or six-and-twenty, and fond of a wandering life, so what should he want of a wife and a flock of bantlings?"

"He seems sad and sober sometimes, and I fancied he might have some domestic trouble to harass him. Don't you think there is something peculiar about him?" asked Helen, remembering Hoffman's hint that her uncle knew his wish to travel incognito, and wondering if he would throw any light upon the matter. But the major's face was impenetrable and his answer unsatisfactory.

"Well, I don't know. Everyone has some worry or other, and as for being peculiar, all foreigners seem more or less so to us, they are so unreserved and demonstrative. I like Hoffman more and more every day, and shall be sorry when I part with him."

"Ludmilla is his sister, then, or he didn't tell uncle the truth. It is no concern of mine; but I wish I knew," thought Helen anxiously, and then wondered why she should care.

A feeling of distrust had taken possession of her and

she determined to be on the watch, for the unsuspicious major would be easily duped, and Helen trusted more to her own quick and keen eye than to his experience. She tried to show nothing of the change in her manner; but Hoffman perceived it, and bore it with a proud patience which often touched her heart, but never altered her purpose.

VII

At Fault

Four weeks went by so rapidly that everyone refused to believe it when the major stated the fact at the breakfast-table, for all had enjoyed themselves so heartily that they had been unconscious of the lapse of time.

"You are not going away, uncle?" cried Amy, with a panic-stricken look.

"Next week, my dear; we must be off, for we've much to do yet, and I promised mamma to bring you back by the end of October."

"Never mind Paris and the rest of it; this is pleasanter. I'd rather stay here—"

There Amy checked herself and tried to hide her face behind her coffee cup, for Casimer looked up in a way that made her heart flutter and her cheeks burn.

"Sorry for it, Amy; but go we must, so enjoy your last week with all your might, and come again next year."

"It will never be again what it is now," sighed Amy; and Casimer echoed the words "next year," as if sadly wondering if the present year would not be his last.

Helen rose silently and went into the garden, for of

late she had fallen into the way of reading and working in the little pavilion which stood in an angle of the wall, overlooking lake and mountains.

A seat at the opposite end of the walk was Amy's haunt, for she liked the sun, and within a week or two something like constraint had existed between the cousins. Each seemed happier apart, and each was intent on her own affairs. Helen watched over Amy's health, but no longer offered advice or asked confidence. She often looked anxious, and once or twice urged the major to go, as if conscious of some danger.

But the worthy man seemed to have been bewitched as well as the young folks, and was quite happy sitting by the plump, placid widow, or leisurely walking with her to the chapel on the hillside.

All seemed waiting for something to break up the party, and no one had the courage to do it. The major's decision took everyone by surprise, and Amy and Casimer looked as if they had fallen from the clouds.

The persistency with which the English lessons had gone on was amazing, for Amy usually tired of everything in a day or two. Now, however, she was a devoted teacher, and her pupil did her great credit by the rapidity with which he caught the language. It looked like pleasant play, sitting among the roses day after day, Amy affecting to embroider while she taught, Casimer marching to and fro on the wide, low wall, below which lay the lake, while he learned his lesson; then standing before her to recite, or lounging on the turf in frequent fits of idleness, both talking and laughing a great deal, and generally forgetting everything but the pleasure of being together. They wrote little notes as exercises— Amy in French, Casimer in English, and each corrected the other's.

All very well for a time; but as the notes increased the corrections decreased, and at last nothing was said of ungrammatical French or comical English and the little notes were exchanged in silence.

As Amy took her place that day she looked forlorn, and when her pupil came, her only welcome was a reproachful—

"You are very late, sir."

"It is fifteen of minutes yet to ten clocks," was Casimer's reply, in his best English.

"Ten o'clock, and leave out 'of' before minutes. How many times must I tell you that?" said Amy, severely, to cover her first mistake.

"Ah, so many times; soon all goes to finish, and I

83

have none person to make this charming English go in my so stupid head."

"What will you do then?"

"I jeter myself into the lake."

"Don't be foolish; I'm dull today, and want to be cheered up; suicide isn't a pleasant subject."

"Good! See here, then—a little *plaisanterie*—what you call joke. Can you will to see it?" and he laid a little pink cocked-hat note on her lap, looking like a mischievous boy as he did so.

"'Mon Casimer Teblinski;' I see no joke;" and Amy was about to tear it up, when he caught it from destruction, and holding it out of reach, said, laughing wickedly—

"The 'mon' is one abbreviation of 'monsieur,' but you put no little—how do you say?—period at the end of him; it goes now in English—'*My* Casimer Teblinski,' and that is of the most charming address."

"Don't exult; that was only an oversight, not a deliberate deception like that you put upon me. It was very wrong and rude, and I shall not forget it."

"*Mon Dieu!* Where have I gone in sinning! I am a *polisson*, as I say each day, but not a villain, I swear to you. Say to me that which I have made of wrong, and I will do penance."

"You told me '*Ma drogha*' was the Polish for 'My pupil,' and let me call you so a long time; I am wiser now," replied Amy, with great dignity.

"Who has said stupidities to you, that you doubt me?" And Casimer assumed an injured look, though his eyes danced with merriment.

"I heard Hoffman singing a Polish song to little Roserl, the burden of which was, '*Ma drogha, Ma drogha,*' and when I asked him to translate it, those two words meant, 'My darling.' How dare you, ungrateful creature that you are!"

As Amy spoke, half-confusedly, half-angrily, Casimer went down upon his knees, with folded hands and penitent face, exclaiming in good English—

"Be merciful to me a sinner. I was tempted, and I could not resist."

"Get up this instant, and stop laughing. Say your lesson, for this will be your last," was the stern reply, though Amy's face dimpled all over with suppressed merriment.

"He rose meekly, but made such sad work with the very "To love," that his teacher was glad to put an end to it, by proposing to read her French to him. It was "Thaddeus of Warsaw," a musty little translation which she had found in the house, and begun for her own amusement. Casimer read a little, seemed interested, and suggested that they read it together, so that he might correct her accent. Amy agreed, and they were in the heart of the sentimental romance, finding it more interesting than most modern readers, for the girl had an improved Thaddeus before her, and the Pole a fairer, kinder Mary Beaufort.

Dangerous times for both, but therein lay the charm; for, though Amy said to herself each night, "Sick, poor, and a foreigner—it can never be," yet each morning she felt, with increasing force, how blank her day would be without him. And Casimer, honorably restraining every word of love, yet looked volumes, and in spite of the glasses, the girl felt the eloquence of the fine eyes they could not entirely conceal.

Today, as she read, he listened with his head leaning on his hand, and though she never had read worse, he made no correction, but sat so motionless she fancied at last that he had actually fallen asleep. Thinking to rouse him, she said in French—

"Poor Thaddeus! Don't you pity him?—alone, poor, sick, and afraid to own his love."

"No, I hate him, the absurd imbecile, with his fine boots and plumes, and tragic airs. He was not to be pitied, for he recovered health, he found fortune, he won his Marie. His sufferings were nothing; there was no fatal blight on him, and he had time and power to conquer his misfortunes, while I—"

Casimer spoke with sudden passion, and pausing abruptly, turned his face away, as if to hide some emotion he was too proud to show.

Amy's heart ached, and her eyes filled, but her voice was sweet and steady, as she said, putting by the book, like one weary of it—

"Are you suffering today? Can we do anything for you? Please let us, if we may."

"You give me all I can receive; no one can help my pain yet; but a time will come when something may be done for me; then I will speak." And, to her great surprise, he rose and left her, without another word.

She saw him no more until evening; then he looked excited, played stormily, and would sing in defiance of danger. The trouble in Amy's face seemed reflected in Helen's, though not a word had passed between them. She kept her eye on Casimer, with an intentness that worried Amy, and even when he was at the instrument Helen stood near him, as if fascinated, watching the slender hands chase one another up and down the keys with untiring strength and skill.

Suddenly she left the room and did not return. Amy was so nervous by that time, she could restrain herself no longer, and slipping out, found her cousin in their chamber, poring over a glove.

"Oh, Nell, what is it? You are so odd tonight I can't understand you. The music excites me, and I'm miserable, and I want to know what has happened," she said, tearfully.

"I've found him!" whispered Helen, eagerly, holding up the glove with a gesture of triumph.

Who?" asked Amy, blinded by her tears.

"The baron."

"Where?—when?" cried the girl, amazed.

"Here, and now."

"Don't take my breath away; tell me quick, or I shall get hysterical."

"Casimer is Sigismund Palsdorf, and no more a Pole than I am," was Helen's answer.

Amy dropped in a heap on the floor, not fainting, but so amazed she had neither strength nor breath left. Sitting by her, Helen rapidly went on—

"I had a feeling as if something was wrong, and began to watch. The feeling grew, but I discovered nothing till today. It will make you laugh; it was so unromantic. As I looked over uncle's things when the laundress brought them this afternoon, I found a collar that was not his. It was marked 'S.P.,' and I at once felt a great desire to know who owned it. The woman was waiting for her money, and I asked her. 'Monsieur Pologne,' she said, for his name is too much for her. She took it into his room, and that was the end of it."

"But it may be another name; the initials only a coincidence," faltered Amy, looking frightened.

"No dear, it isn't; there is more to come. Little Roserl came crying through the hall an hour ago, and I asked what the trouble was. She showed me a prettily-bound prayer-book which she had taken from the Pole's room to play with, and had been ordered by her mother to carry back. I looked into it; no name, but the same coat-of-arms as the glove and the handkerchief. Tonight as he played I examined his hands; they are peculiar, and some of the peculiarities have left traces on the glove. I am sure it is he, for on looking back many things confirm the idea. He says he is a *polisson*, a rogue, fond of jokes, and clever at playing them. The Germans are famous for masquerading and practical jokes; this is one, I am sure, and uncle will be terribly angry if he discovers it."

Casimer was not in the room, the major and Mrs.

Cumberland were sipping tea side by side, and the professors roaming vaguely about. To leave Amy in peace, Helen engaged them both in a lively chat, and her cousin sat by the window trying to collect her thoughts. Someone was pacing up and down the garden, hatless, in the dew.

Amy forgot everything but the danger of such exposure to her reckless friend. His cloak and hat lay on a chair; she caught them up and glided unperceived from the long window.

"You are so imprudent I fear for you, and bring your things," said a timid voice, as the little white figure approached the tall black one, striding down the path tempestuously.

"You to think of me, forgetful of yourself! Little angel of kindness, why do you take such care of me?" cried Casimer, eagerly taking not only the cloak, but the hands that held it.

"I pitied you because you were ill and lonely. You do not deserve my pity, but I forgive that, and would not see you suffer," was the reproachful answer, as Amy turned away.

But he held her fast, saying earnestly—

"What have I done? You are angry. Tell me my fault and I will amend."

"You have deceived me."

"How?"

"Will you own the truth?" and in her eagerness to set her fears at rest, Amy forgot Helen.

"I will."

She could not see his face, but his voice was steady and his manner earnest.

"Tell me, then, is not your true name Sigismund Palsdorf?"

He started, but answered instantly—

"It is not."

"You are not the baron?" cried Amy.

"No; I will swear it if you wish."

"Who, then, are you?"

"Shall I confess?"

"Yes, I entreat you."

"Remember, you command me to speak."

"I do. Who are you?"

"Your lover."

The words were breathed into her ear as softly as ardently, but they startled her so much she could find no reply, and, throwing himself down before her, Casimer poured out his passion with an impetuosity that held her breathless.

"Yes, I love you, and I tell it, vain and dishonorable as it is in one like me. I try to hide it. I say 'it cannot be.' I plan to go away. But you keep me; you are angel-good to me; you take my heart, you care for me, teach me, pity me, and I can only love and die. I know it is folly; I ask nothing; I pray to God to bless you always, and I say, Go, go, before it is too late for you, as now for me!"

"Yes, I must go—it is all wrong. Forgive me. I have been very selfish. Oh, forget me and be happy," faltered Amy, feeling that her only safety was in flight.

"Go! Go!" he cried, in a heart-broken tone, yet still kissed and clung to her hands till she tore them away and fled into the house.

Helen missed her soon after she went, but could not follow for several minutes; then went to their chamber and there found Amy drowned in tears, and terribly agitated.

Soon the story was told with sobs and moans, and despairing lamentations fit to touch a heart of stone.

"I do love him—oh, I do; but I didn't know it till he was so unhappy, and now I've done this dreadful harm. He'll die, and I can't help him, see him, or be anything to him. Oh, I've been a wicked, wicked girl, and never can be happy any more."

Angry, perplexed, and conscience-stricken, for what

now seemed blind and unwise submission to the major, Helen devoted herself to calming Amy, and when at last the poor, broken-hearted little soul fell asleep in her arms, she pondered half the night upon the still unsolved enigma of the Baron Sigismund.

VIII
More Mystery

*

"Uncle, can I speak to you a moment?" said Helen, very gravely, as they left the breakfast-room next morning.

"Not now, my dear, I'm busy," was the hasty reply, as the major shawled Mrs. Cumberland for an early promenade.

Helen knit her brows irefully, for this answer had been given her half a dozen times lately when she asked for an interview. It was evident he wished to avoid all lectures, remonstrances, and explanations; and it was also evident that he was in love with the widow.

"Lovers are worse than lunatics to manage, so it is vain to try to get any help from him," sighed Helen, adding, as her uncle was gallantly leading his stout divinity away into the garden: "Amy has a bad headache, and I shall stay to take care of her, so we can't join your party to Chillon, sir. We have been there once, so you needn't postpone it for us."

"Very well, my dear," and the major walked away, looking much relieved.

As Helen was about to leave the salon Casimer

appeared. A single glance at her face assured him that she knew all, and instantly assuming a confiding, persuasive air that was irresistible, he said, meekly—

"Mademoiselle, I do not deserve a word from you, but it desolates me to know that I have grieved the little angel who is too dear to me. For her sake, pardon that I spoke my heart in spite of prudence, and permit me to send her this."

Helen glanced from the flowers he held to his beseeching face, and her own softened. He looked so penitent and anxious she had not the heart to reproach him.

"I will forgive you and carry your gift to Amy on one condition," she said, gravely.

"Ah, you are kind! Name, then, the condition, I implore you, and I will agree."

"Tell me, then, on your honor as a gentleman, are you not Baron Palsdorf?"

"On my honor as a gentleman, I swear to you I am not."

"Are you, in truth, what you profess to be?"

"I am, in truth, Amy's lover, your devoted servant, and a most unhappy man, with but a little while to live. Believe this and pity me, dearest Mademoiselle Helen."

She did pity him, her eyes betrayed that, and her voice was very kind, as she said—

"Pardon my doubts. I trust you now, and wish with all my heart that it were possible to make you happy. You know it is not; therefore, I am sure you will be wise and generous, and spare Amy further grief by avoiding her for the little time we stay. Promise me this, Casimer."

"I may see her if I am dumb? Do not deny me this. I will not speak, but I must look at my little and dear angel when she is near."

He pleaded so ardently with lips and hands and eager eyes that Helen could not deny him, and when he had poured out his thanks she left him, feeling very tender toward the unhappy young lover, whose passion was so hopeless, yet so warm.

Amy was at breakfast in her room, sobbing and sipping, moaning and munching, for, though her grief was great, her appetite was good, and she was in no mood to see anything comical in cracking eggshells while she bewailed her broken heart, or in eating honey in the act of lamenting the bitterness of her fate.

Casimer would have become desperate had he seen her in the little blue wrapper, with her bright hair loose on her shoulders, and her pretty face wet with tears, as she dropped her spoon to seize his flowers—three dewy roses, one a bud, one half and the other fully blown, making a fragrant record and avowal of the love which she must renounce.

"Oh, my dear boy! How can I give him up, when he is so fond, and I am all he has? Helen, uncle must let me write or go to mamma. She shall decide; I can't; and no one else has a right to part us," sobbed Amy, over her roses.

"Casimer will not marry, dear; he is too generous to ask such a sacrifice," began Helen, but Amy cried indignantly—

"It is no sacrifice; I'm rich. What do I care for his poverty?"

"His religion!" hinted Helen, anxiously. "Surely he is Catholic."

"It need not part us; we can believe what we will. He is good; why mind whether he is Catholic or Protestant?"

"But a Pole, Amy, so different in tastes, habits, character, and beliefs. It is a great risk to marry a foreigner; people are so unlike."

"I don't care if he is a Tartar, a Calmuck, or any of the wild tribes. I love him, he loves me, and no one need object if I don't."

"But, dear, the great and sad objection still remains— his health. He just said he had but a little while to live."

Amy's angry eyes grew dim, but she answered with soft earnestness—

"So much the more need of me to make that little while happy. Think how much he has suffered and done for others; surely I may do something for him. Oh, Nell, can I let him die alone and in exile, when I have both heart and home to give him?"

Helen could say no more; she kissed and comforted the faithful little soul, feeling all the while such sympathy and tenderness that she wondered at herself, for with this interest in the love of another came a sad sense of loneliness, as if she was denied the sweet experience that every woman longs to know.

Amy never could remain long under a cloud, and seeing Helen's tears, began to cheer both her cousin and herself.

"Hoffman said he might live with care, don't you remember? And Hoffman knows the case better than we. Let us ask him if Casimer is worse. You do it; I can't without betraying myself."

"I will," and Helen felt grateful for any pretext to address a friendly word to Karl, who had looked sad of late, and had been less with them since the major became absorbed in Mrs. Cumberland.

Leaving Amy to compose herself, Helen went away to find Hoffman. It was never difficult, for he seemed to divine her wishes and appear uncalled the moment he was wanted. Hardly had she reached her favorite nook in the garden when he approached with letters, and asked with respectful anxiety, as she glanced at and threw them by with an impatient sigh—

"Has mademoiselle any orders? Will the ladies drive, sail, or make a little expedition? It is fine, and mademoiselle looks as if the air would refresh her. Pardon that I make the suggestion."

"No, Hoffman, I don't like the air of this place, and intend to leave as soon as possible." And Helen knit her delicate dark brows with an expression of great determination. "Switzerland is the refuge of political exiles, and I hate plots and disguises; I feel oppressed by some mystery, and mean to solve or break away from it at once."

She stopped abruptly, longing to ask his help, yet withheld by a sudden sense of shyness in approaching the subject, though she had decided to speak to Karl of the Pole.

"Can I serve you, mademoiselle? If so, pray command me," he said, eagerly, coming a step nearer.

"You can, and I intend to ask your advice, for there can be nothing amiss in doing so, since you are a friend of Casimer's."

"I am both friend and confidant, mademoiselle," he answered, as if anxious to let her understand that he knew all, without the embarrassment of words. She looked up quickly, relieved, yet troubled.

"Everything, mademoiselle. Pardon me if this afflicts you; I am his only friend here, and the poor lad sorely needed comfort."

"He did. I am not annoyed; I am glad, for I know you will sustain him. Now I may speak freely, and be equally frank. Please tell me if he is indeed fatally ill?"

"It was thought so some months ago; now I hope. Happiness cures many ills, and since he has loved, he has improved. I always thought care would save him; he is worth it."

Hoffman paused, as if fearful of venturing too far; but Helen seemed to confide freely in him, and said, softly—

"Ah, if it were only wise to let him be happy. It is so bitter to deny love."

"God knows it is!"

The exclamation broke from Hoffman as if an irrepressible impulse wrung it from him.

Helen started, and for a moment neither spoke. She collected herself soonest, and without turning, said, quietly—

"I have been troubled by a strong impression that Casimer is not what he seems. Till he denied it on his honor I believed him to be Baron Palsdorf. Did he speak the truth when he said he was not?"

"Yes, mademoiselle."

"Then, Casimer Teblinski is his real name?"

No answer.

She turned sharply, and added—

"For my cousin's sake, I must know the truth. Several curious coincidences make me strongly suspect that he is passing under an assumed name."

Not a word said Hoffman, but looked on the ground, as motionless and expressionless as a statue.

Helen lost patience, and in order to show how much she had discovered, rapidly told the story of the gloves, ring, handkerchief, prayer-book and collar, omitting all hint of the girlish romance they had woven about these things.

As she ended, Hoffman looked up with a curious expression, in which confusion, amusement, admiration and annoyance seemed to contend.

"Mademoiselle," he said, gravely, "I am about to prove to you that I feel honored by the confidence you place in me. I cannot break my word, but I will confess to you that Casimer does *not* bear his own name."

"I knew it!" said Helen, with a flash of triumph in her eyes. "He *is* the baron, and no Pole. You Germans love masquerades and jokes. This is one, but I must spoil it before it is played out."

"Pardon; mademoiselle is keen, but in this she is mistaken. Casimer is *not* the baron; however, he did fight for Poland, and his name is known and honored there. Of this I solemnly assure you."

She stood up and looked him straight in the face. He met her eye to eye and never wavered till her own fell.

She mused a few minutes, entirely forgetful of herself in her eagerness to solve the mystery.

Hoffman stood so near that her dress touched him, and the wind blew her scarf against his hand; and as she thought he watched her while his eyes kindled, his color rose, and once he opened his lips to speak, but she moved at the instant, and exclaimed—

"I have it!"

"Now for it," he muttered, as if preparing for some new surprise or attack.

"When uncle used to talk about the Polish revolution, there was, I remember, a gallant young Pole who did something brave. The name just flashed on me, and it clears up my doubts. Stanislas Prakora—'S.P.'—and Casimer is the man."

Helen spoke with an eager, bright face, as if sure of the truth now; but, to her surprise, Hoffman laughed, a short, irrepressible laugh, full of hearty but brief merriment. He sobered in a breath, and with an entire change of countenance said, in an embarrassed tone—

"Pardon my rudeness; mademoiselle's acuteness threw me off my guard. I can say nothing till released from my promise; but mademoiselle may rest assured that Casimer Teblinski is as good and brave a man as Stanislas Prakora."

Helen's eyes sparkled, for in this reluctant reply she read confirmation of her suspicion, and thought that Amy would rejoice to learn that her lover was a hero.

"You are exiles, but still hope and plot, and never relinquish your hearts' desire?"

"Never, mademoiselle!"

"You are in danger?"

"In daily peril of losing all we most love and long for," answered Karl, with such passion that Helen found patriotism a lovely and inspiring thing.

"You have enemies?" she asked, unable to control her interest, and feeling the charm of these confidences.

"Alas! yes," was the mournful reply, as Karl dropped his eyes to hide the curious expression of mirth which he could not banish from them.

"Can you not conquer them, or escape the danger they place you in?"

"We hope to conquer; we cannot escape."

"This accounts for your disguise and Casimer's false name?"

"Yes. We beg that mademoiselle will pardon us the anxiety and perplexity we have caused her, and hope that a time will soon arrive when we may be ourselves. I fear the romantic interest with which the ladies have honored us will be much lessened, but we shall still remain their most humble and devoted servants."

Something in his tone nettled Helen, and she said sharply—

"All this may be amusing to you, but it spoils my confidence in others to know they wear masks. Is your name also false?"

"I am Karl Hoffman, as surely as the sun shines, mademoiselle. Do not wound me by a doubt," he said, eagerly.

"And nothing more?"

She smiled as she spoke, and glanced at his darkened

skin with a shake of the head.

"I dare not answer that."

"No matter; I hate titles, and value people for their own worth, not for their rank."

Helen spoke impulsively, and, as if carried away by her words and manner, Hoffman caught her hand and pressed his lips to it ardently, dropped it, and was gone, as if fearing to trust himself a moment longer.

Helen stood where he left her, thinking, with a shy glance from her hand to the spot where he had stood—

"It is pleasant to have one's hand kissed, as Amy said. Poor Karl, his fate is almost as hard as Casimer's."

Some subtle power seemed to make the four young people shun one another carefully, though all longed to be together. The major appeared to share the secret disquiet that made the rest roam listlessly about, till little Roserl came to invite them to a *fete* in honor of the year's vintage. All were glad to go, hoping in the novelty and excitement to recover their composure.

The vineyard sloped up from the chateau, and on the hillside was a small plateau of level sward, shadowed by a venerable oak now hung with garlands, while underneath danced the chateau servants with their families to the music of a pipe played by little Friedel. As the gentlefolk approached, the revel stopped, but the major, who was in an antic mood and disposed to be gracious, bade Friedel play on, and as Mrs. Cumberland refused his hand with a glance at her weeds, the major turned to the Count's buxom housekeeper, and besought her to waltz with him. She assented, and away they went as nimbly as the best. Amy laughed, but stopped to blush, as Casimer came up with an imploring glance, and whispered—

"Is it possible that I may enjoy one divine waltz with you before I go?"

Amy gave him her hand with a glad assent, and Helen was left alone. Everyone was dancing but herself and Hoffman, who stood near by, apparently unconscious of the fact. He glanced covertly at her, and saw that she was beating time with foot and hand, that her eyes shone, her lips smiled. He seemed to take courage at this, for, walking straight up to her, he said, as coolly as if a crown-prince—

"Mademoiselle, may I have the honor?"

A flash of surprise passed over her face, but there was no anger, pride, or hesitation in her manner, as she leaned toward him with a quiet "Thanks, monsieur."

A look of triumph was in his eyes as he swept her away to dance, as she had never danced before, for a German waltz is full of life and spirit, wonderfully captivating to English girls, and German gentlemen make it a memorable experience when they please. As they circled round the rustic ball-room, Hoffman never took his eyes off Helen's, and, as if fascinated, she looked up at him, half conscious that he was reading her heart as she read his. He said not a word, but his face grew very tender, very beautiful in her sight, as she forgot everything except that he had saved her life and she loved him. When they paused, she was breathless and pale; he also; and seating her he went away to bring her a glass of wine. As her dizzy eyes grew clear, she saw a little case at her feet, and taking it up, opened it. A worn paper, containing some faded forget-me-nots and these words, fell out—

"Gathered where Helen sat on the night of August 10th."

There was just time to restore its contents to the case, when Hoffman returned, saw it, and looked intensely annoyed as he asked, quickly—

"Did you read the name on it?"

"I saw only the flowers;" and Helen colored beautifully as she spoke.

"And read *them*?" he asked, with a look she could not meet.

She was spared an answer, for just then a lad came up, saying, as he offered a note—

"Monsieur Hoffman, madame, at the hotel, sends you this, and begs you to come at once."

As he impatiently opened it, the wind blew the paper into Helen's lap. She restored it, and in the act, her quick eye caught the signature, "Thine ever, Ludmilla."

A slight shadow passed over her face, leaving it very cold and quiet. Hoffman saw the change, and smiled, as if well pleased, but assuming suddenly his usual manner, said deferentially—

"Will mademoiselle permit me to visit my friend for an hour? She is expecting me."

"Go, then; we do not need you," was the brief reply, in a careless tone, as if his absence was a thing of no interest to anyone.

"Thanks; I shall not be long away;" and giving her a glance that made her turn scarlet with anger at its undisguised admiration, he walked away, humming gaily to himself Goethe's lines—

"Maiden's heart and city wall
 Were made to yield, were made to fall;
When we've held them each their day,
Soldier-like we march away."

IX

"S.P." and the Baron

Dinner was over, and the salon deserted by all but the two young ladies, who sat apart, apparently absorbed in novels, while each was privately longing for somebody to come, and with the charming inconsistency of the fair sex, planning to fly if certain some bodies *did* appear.

Steps approached; both buried themselves in their books; both held their breath and felt their hearts flutter as they never had done before at the step of mortal man. The door opened; neither looked up, yet each was conscious of mingled disappointment and relief when the major said, in a grave tone, "Girls, I've something to tell you."

"We know what it is, sir," returned Helen, coolly.

"I beg your pardon, but you don't, my dear, as I will prove in five minutes, if you will give me your attention."

The major looked as if braced up to some momentous undertaking; and planting himself before the two young ladies, dashed bravely into the subject.

"Girls, I've played a bold game, but I've won it, and will take the consequences."

"They will fall heaviest on you, uncle," said Helen, thinking he was about to declare his love for the widow.

The major laughed, shrugged his shoulders, and answered, stoutly—

"I'll bear them; but you are quite wrong, my dear, in your surmises, as you will soon see. Helen is my ward, and accountable to me alone. Amy's mother gave her into my charge, and won't reproach me for anything that has passed when I explain matters. As to the lads they must take care of themselves."

Suddenly both girls colored, fluttered, and became intensely interested. The major's eyes twinkled as he assumed a perfectly impassive expression, and rapidly delivered himself of the following thunderbolt—

"Girls, you have been deceived, and the young men you love are impostors."

"I thought so," muttered Helen, grimly.

"Oh, uncle, don't say that!" cried Amy, despairingly.

"It's true, my dears; and the worst of it is, I knew the truth all the time. Now, don't have hysterics, but listen and enjoy the joke as I do. At Coblentz, when you sat in the balcony, two young men overheard Amy sigh for adventures, and Helen advise making a romance out of the gloves one of the lads had dropped. They had seen you by day; both admired you, and being idle, carefree young fellows, they resolved to devote their vacation to gratifying your wishes and enjoying themselves. We met at the Fortress; I knew one of them, and liked the other immensely; so when they confided their scheme to me I agreed to help them carry it out, and I had perfect confidence in both, and thought a little adventure or two would do you good."

"Uncle, you were mad," said Helen; and Amy added, tragically—

"You don't know what trouble has come of it."

"Perhaps I was; that remains to be proved. I do know everything, and fail to see any trouble, so don't cry, little girl," briskly replied the inexplicable major. "Well, we had a merry time planning our prank. One of the lads insisted on playing the courier, though I objected. He'd done it before, liked the part, and would have his way. The other couldn't decide, being younger and more in love; so we left him to come into the comedy when he was ready. Karl did capitally, as you will allow; and I am much attached to him, for in all respects he has been true to his word. He began at Coblentz; the other, after doing the mysterious at Heidelberg, appeared as an exile, and made quick work with the prejudices of my well-beloved nieces—hey, Amy?"

"Go on; who are they?" cried both girls, breathlessly.

"Wait a bit; I'm not bound to expose the poor fellows to your scorn and anger. No; if you are going to be high and haughty, to forget their love, refuse to forgive their frolic, and rend their hearts with reproaches, better let them remain unknown."

"No, no; we will forget and forgive, only speak!" was the command of both.

"You promise to be lenient and mild, to let them confess their motives, and to award a gentle penance for their sins?"

"Yes, we promise!"

"Then, come in, my lads, and plead for your lives."

As he spoke the major threw open the door, and two gentlemen entered the room—one, slight and dark, with brilliant black eyes; the other tall and large, with blond hair and beard. Angry, bewildered, and shame-stricken as they were, feminine curiosity overpowered all other feelings for the moment, and the girls sat looking at the culprits with eager eyes, full of instant recognition; for though the disguise was off, and neither had seen them in their true characters but once, they felt no doubt, and involuntarily exclaimed—

"Karl!"

"Casimer!"

"No, young ladies; the courier and exile are defunct, and from their ashes rise Baron Sigismund Palsdorf, my friend, and Sidney Power, my nephew. I give you one hour to settle the matter; then I shall return to bestow my blessing or to banish these scapegraces forever."

And, having fired his last shot, the major prudently retreated, without waiting to see its effect.

It was tremendous, for it carried confusion into the fair enemy's camp; and gave the besiegers a momentary advantage of which they were not slow to avail themselves.

For a moment the four remained mute and motionless: then Amy, like all timid things, took refuge in flight, and Sidney followed her into the garden, glad to see the allies separated. Helen, with the courage of her nature, tried to face and repulse the foe; but love was stronger than pride, maiden shame overcame anger, and, finding it vain to meet and bear down the steady, tender glance of the blue eyes fixed upon her, she dropped her head into her hands and sat before him, like one conquered but too proud to cry "Quarter." Her lover watched her till she hid her face, then drew near, knelt down before her, and said, with an undertone of deep feeling below the mirthful malice of his words—

"Mademoiselle, pardon me that I am a foolish baron, and dare to offer you the title that you hate. I have served you faithfully for a month, and, presumptuous as it is, I ask to be allowed to serve you all my life. Helen, say you forgive the deceit for love's sake."

"No; you are false and forsworn. How can I believe that anything is true?"

And Helen drew away the hand of which he had taken possession.

"Heart's dearest, you trusted me in spite of my disguise; trust me still, and I will prove that I am neither false nor forsworn. Catechize me, and see if I was not true in spite of all my seeming deception."

"You said your name was Karl Hoffman," began Helen, glad to gain a little time to calm herself before the momentous question came.

"It is; I have many, and my family choose to call me Sigismund," was the laughing answer.

"I'll never call you so; you shall be Karl, the courier, all your life to me," cried Helen, still unable to meet the ardent eyes before her.

"Good; I like that well; for it assures me that all my life I shall be something to you, my heart. What next?"

"When I asked if you were the baron, you denied it."

"Pardon! I simply said my name was Hoffman. You did not ask me point blank if I was the baron; had you done so, I think I should have confessed all, for it was very hard to restrain myself this morning."

"No, not yet; I have more questions;" and Helen warned him away, as it became evident that he no longer considered restraint necessary.

"Who is Ludmilla?" she said, sharply.

"My faith, that is superb!" exclaimed the baron, with a triumphant smile at her betrayal of jealousy. "How if she is a former love?" he asked, with a sly look at her changing face.

"It would cause me no surprise; I am prepared for anything."

"How if she is my dearest sister, for whom I sent, that she might welcome you and bring the greetings of my parents to their new daughter?"

"Is it indeed so?"

And Helen's eyes dimmed as the thought of parents, home and love filled her heart with tenderest gratitude, for she had long been an orphan.

"*Leibchen*, it is true; tomorrow you shall see how dear you already are to them, for I write often and they wait eagerly to receive you."

Helen felt herself going very fast, and made an effort to harden her heart, lest too easy victory should reward this audacious lover.

"I may not go; I also have friends, and in England we are not won in this wild way. I will yet prove you false; it will console me for being so duped if I can call you traitor. You said Casimer had fought in Poland."

"Cruelest of women, he did, but under his own name, Sidney Power."

"Then, he was not the brave Stanislas?—and there is no charming Casimer?"

"Yes, there are both—his and my friends, in Paris; true Poles, and when we go there you shall see them."

"But his illness was a ruse?"

"No; he was wounded in the war and has been ill since. Not a fatal malady, I own; his cough misled you, and *he* had no scruples in fabling to any extent. I am not to bear the burden of his sins."

"Then, the romances he told us about your charity, your virtues, and—your love of liberty were false?" said Helen, with a keen glance, for these tales had done much to interest her in the unknown baron.

Sudden color rose to his forehead, and for the first

time his eyes fell before hers—not in shame, but with a modest man's annoyance at hearing himself praised.

"Sidney is enthusiastic in his friendship, and speaks too well for me. The facts are true, but he doubtless glorified the simplest by his way of telling it. Will you forgive my follies, and believe me when I promise to play and duel no more?"

"Yes."

She yielded her hand now, and her eyes were full of happiness, yet she added, wistfully—

"And the betrothed, your cousin, Minna—is she, in truth, not dear to you?"

"Very dear, but less so than another; for I could not learn of her in years what I learned in a day when I met you. Helen, this was begun in jest—it ends in solemn earnest, for I love my liberty, and I have lost it, utterly and forever. Yet I am glad; look in my face and tell me you believe it."

He spoke now as seriously as fervently, and with no shadow on her own, Helen brushed back the blond hair and looked into her lover's face. Truth, tenderness, power, and candor were written there in characters that could not lie; and with her heart upon her lips, she answered, as he drew her close—

"I do believe, do love you, Sigismund!"

Meanwhile another scene was passing in the garden. Sidney, presuming upon his cousinship, took possession of Amy, bidding her "strike but hear him." Of course she listened with the usual accompaniment of tears and smiles, reproaches and exclamations, varied by cruel exultations and coquettish commands to go away and never dare approach her again.

"*Ma drogha*, listen and be appeased. Years ago you and I played together as babies, and our fond mammas vowed we should one day marry. When I was a youth of fourteen and you a mite of ten I went away to India with my father, and at our parting promised to come back and marry you. Being in a fret because you couldn't go also, you haughtily declined the honor, and when I offered a farewell kiss, struck me with this very little hand. Do you remember it?"

"Not I. Too young for such nonsense."

"I do, and I also remember that in my boyish way I resolved to keep my word sooner or later, and I've done it."

"We shall see, sir," cried Amy, strongly tempted to repeat her part of the childish scene as well as her cousin, but her hand was not free, and he got the kiss without the blow.

"For eleven years we never met. You forgot me, and 'Cousin Sidney' remained an empty name. I was in India till four years ago; since then I've been flying about Germany and fighting in Poland, where I nearly got my quietus."

"My dear boy, were you wounded?"

"Bless you, yes; and very proud of it I am. I'll show you my scars some day; but never mind that now. A while ago I went to England, seized with a sudden desire to find my wife."

"I admire your patience in waiting; so flattering to me, you know," was the sharp answer.

"It looks like neglect, I confess; but I'd heard reports of your flirtations, and twice of your being engaged, so I kept away till my work was done. Was it true?"

"I never flirt, Sidney, and I was only engaged a little bit once or twice. I didn't like it, and never mean to do so any more."

"I shall see that you don't flirt; but you are very much engaged now, so put on your ring and make no romances about any 'S.P.' but myself."

"I shall wait till you clear your character; I'm not going to care for a deceitful impostor. What made you think of this prank?"

"You did."

"I? How?"

"When in England I saw your picture, though you were many a mile away, and fell in love with it. Your mother told me much about you, and I saw she would not frown upon my suit. I begged her not to tell you I had come, but let me find you and make myself known when I liked. You were in Switzerland, and I went after you. At Coblentz I met Sigismund, and told him my case; he is full of romance, and when we overheard you in the balcony we were glad of the hint. Sigismund was with me when you came, and admired Helen immensely, so he was wild to have a part in the frolic. I let him begin, and followed you unseen to Heidelberg, meaning to personate an artist. Meeting you at the castle, I made a good beginning with the vaults and the ring, and meant to follow it up by acting the baron, you were so bent on finding him, but Sigismund forbade it. Turning over a trunk of things left there the year before, I came upon my old Polish uniform, and decided to be a Thaddeus."

"How well you did it! Wasn't it hard to act all the time?" asked Amy, wonderingly.

"Very hard with Helen, she is so keen, but not a bit

so with you, for you are such a confiding soul anyone could cheat you. I've betrayed myself a dozen times, and you never saw it. Ah, it was capital fun to play the forlorn exile, study English, and flirt with my cousin."

"It was very base. I should think you'd be devoured with remorse. Aren't you sorry?"

"For one thing. I cropped my head lest you should know me. I was proud of my curls, but I sacrificed them all to you."

"Peacock! Did you think that one glimpse of your black eyes and fine hair would make such an impression that I should recognize you again?"

"I did, and for that reason disfigured my head, put on a mustache, and assumed hideous spectacles. Did you never suspect my disguise, Amy?"

"No. Helen used to say that she felt something was wrong, but I never did till the other night."

"Didn't I do that well? I give you my word it was all done on the spur of the minute. I meant to speak soon, but had not decided how, when you came out so sweetly with that confounded old cloak, of which I'd no more need than an African has of a blanket. Then a scene I'd read in a novel came into my head, and I just repeated it *con amore*. Was I very pathetic and tragical, Amy?"

"I thought so then. It strikes me as ridiculous now, and I can't help feeling sorry that I wasted so much pity on a man who—"

"Loves you with all his heart and soul. Did you cry and grieve over me, dear little tender thing? And do you think now that I am a heartless fellow, bent only on amusing myself at the expense of others? It's not so; and you shall see how true and good and steady I can be when I have anyone to love and care for me. I've been alone so long it's new and beautiful to be petted, confided in, and looked up to by an angel like you."

He was in earnest now; she felt it, and her anger melted away like dew before the sun.

"Poor boy! You will go home with us now, and let us take care of you in quiet England. You'll play no more pranks, but go soberly to work and do something that shall make me proud to be your cousin, won't you?"

"If you'll change 'cousin' to 'wife' I'll be and do whatever you please. Amy, when I was a poor, dying, Catholic foreigner you loved me and would have married me in spite of everything. Now that I'm your well, rich, Protestant cousin, who adores you as that Pole never could, you turn cold and cruel. Is it because the romance is gone, or because your love was only a girl's fancy, after all?"

"You deceived me and I can't forget it; but I'll try," was the soft answer to his reproaches.

"Are you disappointed that I'm not a baron?"

"A little bit."

"Shall I be a count? They gave me a title in Poland, a barren honor, but all they had to offer, poor souls, in return for a little blood. Will you be Countess Zytomar and get laughed at for your pains, or plain Mrs. Power, with a good old English name?"

"Neither, thank you; it's only a girlish fancy, which will soon be forgotten. Does the baron love Helen?" asked Amy, abruptly.

"Desperately, and she?"

"I think he will be happy; she is not one to make confidantes, but I know by her tenderness with me, her sadness lately, and something in her way of brightening when he comes, that she thinks much of him and loves Karl Hoffman. How it will be with the baron I cannot say."

"No fear of him; he wins his way everywhere. I wish I were as fortunate;" and the gay young gentleman heaved an artful sigh and coughed the cough that always brought such pity to the girl's soft eyes.

She glanced at him as he leaned pensively on the low wall, looking down into the lake, with the level rays of sunshine on his comely face and figure. Something softer than pity stole into her eye, as she said, anxiously—

"You are not really ill, Sidney?"

"I have been, and still need care, else I may have a relapse," was the reply of this treacherous youth, whose constitution was as sound as a bell.

Amy clasped her hands, as if in a transport of gratitude, exclaiming, fervently—

"What a relief it is to know that you are not doomed to—"

She paused with a shiver, as if the word were too hard to utter, and Sidney turned to her with a beaming face, which changed to one of mingled pain and anger, as she added, with a wicked glance—

"Wear spectacles."

"Amy, you've got no heart!" he cried, in a tone that banished her last doubt of his love and made her whisper tenderly, as she clung to his arm—

"No, dear; I've given it all to you."

Punctual to the minute, Major Erskine marched into the salon, with Mrs. Cumberland on his arm, exclaiming, as he eyed the four young people together again—

"Now, ladies, is it to be 'Paradise Lost' or 'Regained' for the prisoners at the bar?"

At this point the astonished gentleman found himself taken possession of by four excited individuals, for the girls embraced and kissed him, the young men wrung his hand and thanked him, and all seemed bent on assuring him that they were intensely happy, grateful and affectionate.

From this assault he emerged flushed and breathless, but beaming with satisfaction, and saying paternally—

"Bless you, my children, bless you. I hoped and worked for this, and to prove how well I practice what I preach, let me present to you—my wife."

As he drew forward the plump widow with a face full of smiles and tears, a second rush was made, and congratulations, salutes, exclamations and embraces were indulged in to everyone's satisfaction.

As the excitement subsided the major said, simply—

"We were married yesterday at Montreaux. Let me hope that you will prove as faithful as I have been, as happy as I am, as blest as I shall be. I loved this lady in my youth, have waited many years, and am rewarded at last, for love never comes too late."

The falter in his cheery voice, the dimness of his eyes, the smile on his lips, and the gesture with which he returned the pressure of the hand upon his arm, told the little romance of the good major's life more eloquently than pages of fine writing, and touched the hearts of those who loved him.

"I have been faithful for eleven years. Give me my reward soon, won't you, dear?" whispered Sidney.

"Don't marry me tomorrow, and if mamma is willing I'll think about it by and by," answered Amy.

"It is beautiful! Let us go and do likewise," said Sigismund to his betrothed.

But Helen, anxious to turn the thoughts of all from emotions too deep for words, drew from her pocket a small pearl-colored object, which she gave to Amy with mock solemnity, as she said, turning to lay her hand again in her lover's—

"Amy, our search is over. *You* may keep the gloves; *I* have the baron."

ABOUT THE EDITOR

Stephen Hines has published both fiction and poetry but is best known as a "literary prospector" who has brought back forgotten works by famous children's author Laura Ingalls Wilder, and works by Louisa May Alcott, and Sir Arthur Conan Doyle. His researches have taken him from the Herbert Hoover Library in West Branch, Iowa, to correspondence with British researchers dealing with the works of Sir Arthur Conan Doyle in the United Kingdom. More than half a million copies of books he has collected and edited are in print, and he has had three bestsellers: *Little House in the Ozarks*, "I *Remember Laura*," and *The Quiet Little Woman*. He continues to write fiction and poetry and has been a newspaper humor columnist for seven years.